The

Cursed

By R.K. Ryals

Copyright © Regina K. Ryals, 2013
All rights reserved.

This is a work of fiction. Names, characters, places, and incidents are products of the author's imagination or are used fictitiously and are not to be construed as real. Any resemblance to actual events, locales, organizations, or persons, living or dead, is entirely coincidental.

Acknowledgements

This book and every book I write would not be possible without some amazing people. To my husband who puts up with my crazy writing habits, strange hours, and coffee addiction. To my sister, Sabrina Williams, who answers her phone at midnight ready to read anything I send her way. To my personal assistant, Christina Silcox, for her friendship, and her remarkable ability to keep me organized and ready to write. To Laura Wright Laroche who diligently produces the cover art and book trailers for my books. To Melissa Wright for patiently putting up with my incessant emails, for her criticism, her conversation, and her friendship. To Elise Marion, an amazing friend and author who gives criticism when needed and is willing to beta read at the drop of a hat. To my amazing fans, and to the spectacular Young Adult and Teen Readers group run by Derinda Love and Jodie O'Brien for the never ending support and friendship they give to every writer they know. To my wonderful "adopter" Shanna Roberson for everything she does. Her awesomeness is beyond words. To Amy McCool, Bree Foster-High, Nanette Del Valle Bradford, Katherine Pegg Eccleston, Heather Andrews, Cara Crabtree, and Carole Ronneberg, you have no idea what it means to me. To Audrey Welch, best friend extraordinaire, who takes me on coffee dates and hides me in book stores for a much needed respite. Life wouldn't be the same without you. And last, but never least, to all of the bloggers, fans, and friends who follow me in life, on facebook, on twitter, and anywhere else I may be with amazing support and encouraging words. You mean the world to me.

In the Shadows, there is death. A witch must always follow the Rede. If he turns his back on it, he will be met with darkness, with evil. For with great magic comes great responsibility.

~The Ayers Grimoire~

Chapter 1

My best friend has been bound to a Demon! A Demon! When she told me, I almost laughed. I mean, she was hysterical, and she looked sick. And then, while sitting at the library, she lost it. Really lost it, mumbling things no sane person would believe. Luckily for her, I don't really consider myself sane. My visions have put me in the freak category. And I had seen Dayton bound by chains in a vision. Chains and blood ... Oh, my God! We're both insane.

~Monroe's Totally Wicked Book of Shadows~

"A witch, is a witch, is a witch, is a witch ..."

The screeching was causing a migraine, and I winced.

"They make special places for voices like yours, NeeCee."

If I sounded irate, it was because I meant to sound that way.

My sixteen year-old cousin, Bernice Woodward Ayers, looked up from behind the checkout counter of her mother's *Southern Charms* shop, a boutique of paranormal paraphernalia, and blinked at me owlishly.

"American Idol?" she asked hopefully.

I hated to burst her bubble, but she had enough problems without me raising her expectations.

"No," I answered. "It's called a pillow against the mouth."

I was *not* being mean. Mean was her mother giving her the name Bernice Woodward. Sometimes it's okay *not* to pass down a family name. Just saying. It's why I called her NeeCee. Not much better than Bernice but definitely *better*.

Mean was her mother letting her pick out huge, gaudy brown frames for the glasses she wore now when they clashed badly with her long, strawberry blonde hair and thin face.

Mean was her mother telling her she was ready to join the Pierre de Lune Coven, which in English simply means moonstone. According to my aunt, moonstone sounded so much more romantic in French. But no matter how romantic it sounded, it didn't change the fact that Bernice was *not* ready to cast spells. For one thing, anything she attempted didn't just simply fail, it backfired. *Seriously* backfired.

"You're one to talk, Roe," Bernice grumbled as she flipped through a fashion magazine with all the gusto of a potato interested in being peeled.

NeeCee wasn't a bad sort. She was just lonely. I think, in the long run, my aunt wanted a debutante for a daughter who liked wearing clothes from Alloy and Body Central, not an intellectual whose idea of fun was memorizing the herbs that came into the shop. It didn't help that NeeCee didn't have a magical talent yet either. Unless one counted accidentally changing red dye to blue.

"You'd look good in this, you know?" NeeCee said as she turned the magazine toward me.

The page was a collection of stretch jeans and belted tops. I cringed inwardly. I might tease Bernice for her differences, but I had plenty of my own.

Born Ellie Elizabeth Jacobs, I had changed my

own name to Monroe as a child due to my affection for film star Marilyn Monroe. It was my mother's fault really. Mom had a thing for black and white movies which had fed my love for all things vintage. Modern clothes could take a dive in the dirt and roll in it for all I cared. The baby blue knee-length dress and platforms I had on now was a clear indicator of my fashion sense. And that didn't include the headband holding back my bobbed light blonde hair.

"You should tell your mom to trash that crap."

My honesty tended to be brutal. Bernice rolled her eyes and turned the page back around.

"Having any luck with the grimoire?" Bernice asked, her gaze on the leather-bound book in my hands.

I sighed. Most of my mother's family were Wiccans, and the Ayers grimoire was a massive tome filled with centuries of our family's history, spells, recipes, experiments, talents ... you name it, but I was interested in only one thing. Demonology.

I was fifteen years-old when I had my first vision. It had been a waking dream of a distant cousin who had died two days later from an illness no one could explain. The vision had been vague, ambiguous enough I couldn't offer any explanation of my own, and it had shaken me. It had been the beginning of my abilities.

A year later, I'd had another massive insight. This one had involved my best friend, Dayton Blainey. In the revelation, she had been covered in chains and blood. Within a week, her fanatically religious aunt had bound her to a blood-sucking hybrid Demon. And while Dayton's story eventually worked itself out, I discovered something about myself through her journey. I had the uncanny ability of tapping into Demonic energy. I had even managed to craft amulets that could fend off Demonic possession. As handy as this was, it was also dangerous. Why? Demons now wanted me dead.

Hence the reason I now found myself in my aunt's New Orleans shop, flipping through Ayers' history, and being forced to live upstairs with *said* aunt and *badly named* cousin while the *romantically dubbed* Coven attempted to discover a way to sever my ties with Demonic powers. We weren't having much luck. For one thing, we had yet to discover a spell or a witch with the power to strip me of my so-called curse.

Witches with real magical abilities are often misunderstood. We don't always *need* spells. Certain objects, such as moonstones, can amplify magic, but we don't require incantations unless what we need is outside the realm of our individual abilities. Our magic is all about control, learning how to manage whatever energy we were born with. Circles, magical objects, and spells were for the benefit of the Coven, for members who didn't have powers but practiced Wicca, and for members who had magic but needed to use gifts they didn't have.

"Can I see that?" NeeCee asked suddenly, and I looked up to find her standing over me, her hand outstretched, her gaze on the grimoire.

I narrowed my eyes. "Why?"

NeeCee sighed. "I think I know something that may help you."

I felt myself start to panic and tamped it down. The only thing worse than dust (I'm a slight neat freak) was Bernice's gift for inadvertently abusing magic.

"I don't know— "

"Oh for God's sake!" NeeCee said irritably before snatching the book out of my hand.

I tried grabbing for it and failed.

"NeeCee ..." I warned.

She ignored me, dancing around different glass displays, her eyes on the book. She was naturally clumsy, but inside a store she'd practically been born into, she had the grace of a gazelle. It worked against me.

She paused abruptly, twisting so that her stomach was against a display of dried herbs, her index finger moving down a page. The display between us was too thick for me to see the parchment clearly, and I started edging toward her, my heart beating fast.

"NeeCee ..." I warned again, my teeth gritted.

She grinned. "Look! It's a reversal spell. This could help, you know. And it's simple."

She lifted a candle from a cabinet behind her and lit it. It was black.

Crap!

I blew the wick out.

"No!" I cried. "There is no way in hell I am letting you perform anything on me. Understand?"

Bernice frowned, her forehead creased. "You really have that little confidence in me?"

I could hear the hurt in her voice, and I felt a pang of sympathy. Truly I did, but I wasn't about to let it affect my judgment.

"I have plenty of confidence in you, NeeCee, but these are old spells. They are unpredictable. *Extremely* unpredictable."

Bernice lit the candle again and moved it behind her, her finger trailing the page. She turned, facing me.

"Quae mea tua sunt, tua mea sunt quid . . ." she proceeded stubbornly, her chin raised, her eyes large and confident behind her spectacles.

The words were Latin. I recognized them instantly and cringed, jumping onto the display case, my blue dress riding all the way up to my hip. At this point, I didn't give a flip if a customer came in right now and got an eye full of my black low-rise panties. I just wanted the dead blasted grimoire.

"NeeCee, no!" I shouted, just as the black candle behind her exploded, ebony wax falling onto the wooden surface around it.

I covered my face, but even though the blast sounded loud inside the store, there was no collateral damage. The only outwardly disturbing sign was a small, perfect wax circle made of six black spots on the worn wood around the scarlet glass candleholder. I winced. Bernice froze.

"NeeCee," I whispered.

"Yeah?" she muttered.

I stared at the ruined workstation as the grimoire fell to the floor at Bernice's feet. "That wasn't a reversal spell."

She didn't answer me, but I knew as well as she that her Latin was weak. She was a pure genius with numbers and logical magic, but this ... *this* ...

"What—" she began.

I spun and faced her, my face a mask of rage.

"Which I have is yours, yours is mine ..." I translated, letting the words fade as NeeCee's face lost color.

She knew what the words meant.

"Monroe," she pleaded just as the door to the shop *dinged*.

We both looked up, our eyes landing on my aunt's pink-clad back as she dragged in a box labeled "statues," her breath ragged as she moved. It was a specialty order from a local witch with a talent in glass blowing and handmade pottery.

NeeCee looked back at me, her eyes beseeching.

"Monroe," she begged.

Aunt Clara stood up, dusted her hands off on her pants, and exhaled, her blonde bangs lifting from her flushed face. My willowy aunt was a very, *very* good friend of color. Presently, her silky hair was offset by a pink pantsuit and dangling pink purse. A butterfly sewn on her buttoned-up top sparkled at me, taunting me in an "I dare you to stick your finger down your throat and gag" fashion. I was so *not* a pink fan. Personally, anything that resembles the color of Pepto Bismol should be reserved specifically for vomiting.

As soon as Clara's gaze met ours, her eyes narrowed. "Everything okay in here girls?"

NeeCee scooted carefully in front of the candle, and I had to pinch myself on the leg to keep from bellowing about Bernice's total magical ineptitude. It was a serious lesson in patience and fortitude.

"Just fine," I mumbled.

If we couldn't figure out how to reverse whatever damage NeeCee had caused with the grimoire's spell, I was going to make sure she got taken through the ringer. Maybe even burned at the stake. Or hung. There were Hunters out there who still did that even now.

Aunt Clara used her foot to shove the box to the side of the door before moving toward us.

"Something tells me it's best not to ask. If you two are fighting, work it out. I've got a meeting with Belle in ten minutes in the back." Clara's gaze moved to Bernice. "There are a few things that need to be unboxed and moved from the storage room upstairs."

Bernice nodded, her face pale as her mother's eyes moved to mine.

"Mind the store for a few minutes? I need to confer with the Coven, but I think I may have another formula we can try on you."

I swallowed hard. "If you suggest eating any sort of weird, previously extinct animal remains, I will barf now and save you the trouble."

My aunt glared at me, but she'd be lying if she said the brew she'd tried to make me drink the night before didn't contain some sort of animal entrails. I'd flatly refused.

"This problem you have is daunting, Roe. At this point, we'll try anything."

Her words cut me. Calling me daunting was worse than calling me a freak or an anomaly. If I were a freak, I'd only be a danger to myself. I could handle that. Daunting in thesaurus terms
is the same thing as scary, disheartening, intimidating, and overwhelming. I was *daunting* because my connection with Demons was a risk to my entire family. Handling that was out of the question.

Daunting was the reason why I chose not to argue as Aunt Clara gave me one final perusal before exiting through a door into the back. Compared to the store, the back rooms, used for rituals and readings, were large and mostly bare.

"Thank you," NeeCee whispered as she quickly scraped the candle from the table, using her fingernails to pry off the six wax dots.

I pointed a finger at her face.

"Nah ah! Don't you dare thank me, Bernice Woodward! Not until you go upstairs, start digging through the grimoire for the spell you did, and find a way to fix it. Until then, I'm having murderous thoughts that requires groveling not gratitude."

NeeCee took me seriously, shoving the fallen grimoire under her arm as she scurried to a door that opened onto a set of wrought iron stairs. She paused only once, seemed to rethink whatever she planned to say, and then gently closed the door behind her. I was left alone in the shop, my thoughts whirring.

If Bernice had done the incantation I was sure she'd done, then we were in a hell of a lot of trouble. To begin with, my aunt wouldn't need to be feeding *me* anymore so-called formulas. She would need to be feeding Bernice. Because if I was right, and I was almost certain

I was, NeeCee had performed a power swap spell.

Chapter 2

A Demon. I'm still trying to process it all. My best friend and a Demon bound by blood. That should be bad enough, but now after meeting the Demon she's bound to, I've discovered it gets worse. I can feel Demons. Really feel them. And it hurts. It feels worse than when I stuck my finger in a light socket when I was six (my brothers and their stupid dares). It makes me want to hide, to pretend there aren't such things as monsters, but I've never been good at hiding. Whether I like it or not, I'm no longer just a witch. I'm a Demon lightning rod. And I'm pretty sure I'm not being overly dramatic.

~Monroe's Totally Wicked Book of Shadows~

"*I* want him dead!" the woman yelled passionately and with dramatic, senseless gusto.

What's with that, anyway? It was always dramatically and with a fanaticism I felt the situation never actually warranted. There must be some club somewhere committed to the overhaul of rich husbands. My aunt got some really messed up customers.

"Dead!" she repeated, my eyes crossing reflexively as she waved a grainy photograph frantically in front of my nose.

"Oh, geez! Get real! This called for backup—of the chocolate variety no doubt, and I reached inconspicuously for the bag full of Hershey's kisses stuffed on the top shelf of the counter where I stood. Peeking quickly, I managed to get one snatched, unwrapped, and in my mouth before the photograph once again committed a hit and run with my face. This time, I grabbed for it just as it crashed with my nose.

"Your husband, I presume?" I asked, as I glanced at the smiling, flirtatious gentleman in the photo.

It was amazing how alike they all looked. Like the Stepford wives, only with the wrong equipment, if you know what I mean. And it was the usual scenario—middle-aged businessman, half hanging out of a luxury vehicle while smiling with promising ease at a figure just out of camera shot. Couldn't people be more creative? I don't know, throw a wrench in the mix somewhere. Maybe add a UFO or an alien or two.

"I want him dead!" the woman repeated.

I sighed sullenly around the chocolate piece of heaven tucked within my mouth.

"That much I get," I muttered.

She was babbling now, on and on about some such nonsense, but I lost her somewhere between her first squeal and the big alligator tears. *Dead.* They always wanted them dead. Can anyone say life insurance? If I was promised a cut from every woman who'd entered this shop since I'd arrived two months ago with the same
preoccupied "please kill him" statement, I'd be on my way to one very wealthy 18 year-old girl right now, living it up on some deserted, purchased island in the middle of nowhere with Paul Walker rubbing lotion into my back.

"Are you listening to me?" the woman asked suddenly, snapping me rudely from my self-absorbed day dream just as Paul was about to lean over and ...

" You do realize that committing murder, no matter

how it is accomplished, is an illegal act, Mrs. ... ummm ..."

My sentence trailed off as I realized that somewhere within her monologue, I'd missed the introductions. She glared unobtrusively at my figure, taking in my somewhat tall stature, short blonde hair, and light blue eyes in a head to toe examination that left me feeling invaded. She should have seen me this morning. It had been much, *much* worse.

"Davidson. Mrs. Davidson. You'd be aware of that if you'd been listening," she remarked, giving me a hard look. "And, yes, I am well aware of the law. My husband is, after all, a lawyer."

I bit back a laugh. Weren't they always? Doctors, lawyers, real estate magnates ... it was always the same. I rolled my eyes before reaching behind me to grab the alternative I'd learned to use when dealing with scorned women, a small twinge of compassion filling me for the man it would eventually affect. And then I looked at Mrs. Davidson and lost all semblance of pity. Any man who'd marry this woman and then cheat on her in the first place deserved a wakeup call.

"Why not an alternative?" I asked smoothly, laying the strange looking doll on the countertop as Mrs. Davidson raised a brow.

"Will it kill him?"

She was a very determined woman, our Mrs. Davidson.

"Killing him is a little blasé, don't you think. This way, you get the vengeance you want and he's stuck with the suffering."

I demonstrated the many uses the voodoo-looking doll I'd produced could affect on the person it targeted. The doll actually had nothing to do with voodoo. It was charmed by my aunt, a form of grey magic that caused minor, mostly embarrassing, calamities to the person it was used against. Think hair loss or impotence.

Mrs. Davidson seemed impressed but not wholly convinced. And I was almost out of Hershey's kisses. In other words, my patience was *goooone*.

"It won't kill him?" she asked again, staring in fascination at the little doll smiling wickedly in her direction. Darn, but she was dense!

I picked up the doll while reaching for the bag of chocolate and yelped when my hand met human hair instead.

"Jesus!"

My heart pounded as I glanced down, my eyes meeting the forest green irises of a dark-haired man. I recognized him instantly and my blood ran cold. Luther Craig. Luther flipping Craig!

He was sitting, leaning casually against the counter, one leg propped, his arm flung across it. His other hand rested against the floor. His black hair gleamed blue in the fluorescent lighting.

"Try again, Witch," he mouthed, one brow cocked, his full lips quirked.

The suave Luther Craig. Luther Craig, hybrid Demon. Luther Craig, the son of a she-Demon named Lilith and the notorious cursed Cain, son of Adam and Eve. Luther Craig, the brother of the Demon my best friend, Dayton, was bound to. Luther dead blamed Craig, a man I thought I'd never see again.

The two of us didn't actually have much of a past together. It was more like a sole moment in time. Most of the history we shared revolved around his brother, Marcas, and my bestie, Dayton, but there was one occasion no one knew about, one *single* occurrence when during Dayton's adventure we'd been left alone following Marcas and Dayton's escape from Italy and before the arrival of a fallen Angel named Lucas. A single, lone, solitary moment that still haunted me.

"Do I frighten you, Witch?"

I leaned away from Luther, backing up until my shoulders were against the door of my temporary bedroom at S.O.S. headquarters.

"No," I answered.

We both knew by the way my voice wavered I was lying.

"How did you do it?" he asked.

I knew he meant the amulet I was wearing, the same necklace I had gifted Dayton before she and Marcas had left, the same necklace I had given her right before Luther supposedly disappeared. And yet here he was, and no one knew he was here.

"I don't know what you mean."

His hand came to rest next to my head, his face only inches away from mine.

"Don't play games with me, Witch. I'm not the good guy here. Understand? If you want good, scream. There's a fallen Angel downstairs who'd be glad to rescue you."

Lucas was an Exiled Angel who had shown up to talk to the head of the S.O.S., a society that protected certain religious artifacts, mainly those once used by King Solomon in the Bible. My father and two of my brothers worked for the S.O.S. It was strange really considering me, my mother, and my third oldest brother were all Wiccans. But it worked.

"You won't harm me," I said confidently.

Luther's eyes narrowed. "How did you do it?"

His eyes bore into mine, and I lost the staring contest, turning my head away to glance down the hall.

"I don't know."

I was being honest. My magic was strange. I didn't understand it. All I knew was that when Luther or any other Demons were near me, I could "feel" their energy.

It crackled, like electricity, and the more powerful they were, the more it hurt to be near them. And yet ... I fed off of it. By accident, I had learned standing next to a Demon made it easier for me to perform my own magic. I had also figured out how to block it.

One day, while clutching a piece of quartz, I had pierced my skin with the crystal, allowing the resulting blood to mingle with the gem as I called on my ability, using it to block the electric energy I felt when I was around a Demon. What I had not counted on was the strength caused by mixing quartz, blood, and power. It kept a Demon from possessing me, from possessing anyone who wore an amulet produced the same way.

Luther watched me, his eyes searching before finally pushing away from the wall. I took a deep breath.

"I want an amulet," he ordered.

I stared at him. "Excuse me?"

He looked amused. "I'm pretty sure I didn't stutter."

There was a bad movie joke there, and I was prepared to make one, but one look at the Demon's eyes and I knew it wasn't a good idea.

"Why?" I asked instead.

Luther leaned in again. "I wonder if you know how appealing you are, Ms. Jacobs. Your blood is hard to resist. So, let's make a trade. You give me an amulet, and I'll promise not to kill you. Got it?"

I gasped. I knew the sons of Lilith and Cain craved blood. They were like the mythical vampires with the exception that they didn't need blood to survive. They just liked it.

"I'm not afraid," I whispered.

"The amulet," Luther insisted.

His green eyes suddenly shone red, and I looked away again, pulling a piece of twine away from my neck. I pulled it over my head, cursing myself for my weakness. I did fear him, but I was stronger than that. My instincts were telling me to give him the necklace, and I trusted my instincts.

As soon as the quartz touched Luther's palm, he winced before pulling the makeshift amulet over his head. It landed against his black t-shirt.

"I appreciate that," he said wryly, before leaning so that both his hands trapped me against the door. "You're a strong one, Witch. I can feel it."

One moment, his red eyes watched me, the next his lips were pressed brutally against mine. It was painful, it was brief, and it sent shivers all the way down to my toes.

He pulled away. "For the amulet," he said wickedly.

And with that, he disappeared.

"You okay, girl?"

Mrs. Davidson's impatient voice broke into the memory, and I placed the spelled doll quickly in front of the register, my hands
shaking as I tried to ignore the Demon at my feet.

I wasn't doing a good job. It was hard to pretend an over six foot male in dark blue jeans, and a black leather trench coat wasn't sitting confidently a few inches from my leg. And I was wearing a dress!

"L-look, Mrs. Davidson, we deal in a lot of things at *Southern Charms* but murder is not one of them. It's either the doll or you can leave here, procure a hit man, and cash in the life insurance I just know you're itching to get your hands on."

I was being cynical, but trapped between a murderous woman and an Adonis Demon, cynical seemed tame.

Mrs. Davidson didn't miss a beat. "I'll take it."

"That'll be 12.50 then, I muttered before bagging

the product and handing it to her.

People like Mrs. Davidson really got under my skin. She was, after all, only asking for trouble in the long run. Revenge eventually came back on those who sought it three-fold. No need to point that out though. I had $12.50 in the cash register and a Demon sitting behind the counter. I was not accountable for what happened to the woman once she left the store. Life would be so much simpler if people weren't so interested in the dark arts.

"Have a good day," I said as Mrs. Davidson exited the shop in a dignified fashion belying her reason for stopping by.

"I'm trying to decide whether or not to remark on your current choice of employment or your delightful choice in underwear," Luther's deep voice drawled from the floor as the front door *dinged* closed.

I stiffened, reaching for a feather duster lying on the counter before attempting to clock him upside the head. He moved out of reach, his inhuman speed intimidating as he suddenly stood across from me, the counter between us.

"Seriously?" I asked, still brandishing the duster, my hands tight to keep from trembling. "What the devil are you doing here?"

Chapter 3

Today, I met Luther Craig. It's really all I know to write. He's a Demon, and I can't keep him out of my head. Sure, he's handsome, but I don't think that's it. There's something about him. He's arrogant and scary, but beneath all of that, I see something even more terrifying. I see myself.

~Monroe's Totally Wicked Book of Shadows~

The door leading upstairs opened before Luther had a chance to answer, but his eyes stayed locked on mine, red glinting on green. I didn't have to see NeeCee to know she was in the room with us, and I refused to look her way.

"Monroe?" NeeCee asked.

I raised a hand to silence her just as Luther's eyes narrowed.

"What did you do?" he asked.

I knew he felt the change in energy, knew he could tell that my powers were no longer tied to Demons. It's why I hadn't *felt* him arrive. It confirmed my suspicions. NeeCee had done a power swap spell. We had switched magic.

"I won't let you hurt her," I said quietly.

Luther took a few steps backward, the leather trench coat he wore moving around his legs as he glanced between my spectacled wide-eyed cousin and me.

His lips quirked. "Well, this is a complication."

NeeCee's face was now completely ashen. I knew the pain she was feeling, the electrical charge that was rippling even now through her body. Luther was strong. His power hurt.

"He's a Demon," NeeCee whispered, her awed words directed at me as she edged my way, her back staying near the wall.

"He's a Neanderthal. Being a Demon makes it worse," I muttered, feeling foolish now as I let the feather duster fall to the counter.

Luther shot me a look.

NeeCee gasped. "God, how do you stand it, Roe? It hurts."

NeeCee was speaking as if Luther wasn't in the room. She was scared. She did that when she was afraid.

Luther stepped forward again, his hands on the counter, his eyes on mine. "What *did* you do?"

I didn't flinch. "It was a power swap spell. An accident. My cousin has my powers now, and I hers." Luther cursed, and I leaned forward. "Why does it matter, *Demon*? What are you doing here?"

Luther sighed, pulling the *stolen* amulet around his neck out from under his shirt, letting it land on the black fabric, the glow obvious. NeeCee sighed in relief. It helped with the charge between them.

"I owe your friend, Dayton, for helping my brother," Luther said. "And you, Witch, are in trouble."

I watched him, unease invading my gut. "Dayton sent you?" I asked.

He laughed shortly. "Not exactly. Warned me away to be exact, but the inept fallen Angel they have watching you is not capable of handling what's coming your way."

My eyes widened. Fallen Angel? As in Lucas? Watching *me*? For how long?

NeeCee was at my side now, her presence obvious behind me. "Demons *and* Fallen Angels?" NeeCee hissed in my ear.

I ignored her. "What's coming my way?" I asked.

Luther grinned then. "Hellhounds."

I swallowed hard. I had only seen a Hellhound once, but it was enough. They were terrifying creatures. The size of a horse, muscular, with black, sharp fur and sickly green eyes that shone red when they were furious. They smelled rancid, like sulfur, and they emitted smoke and flame from jaws made to kill. They were escorts and guardians of Hell, sent to bring souls to the Underworld.

"Why?" I whispered.

Luther stared at me, no answer forthcoming. It was a stupid question. I knew why. I had stood before Lucifer once and kept him from possessing Luther in order to use the hybrid
against innocent people. I had given amulets to Satan's enemies to keep the Devil from messing with them. I was pretty sure there were nice, large Wanted posters of me all over Hell.

"It's nice to know you consider me so incompetent, Demon," a male voice broke in wryly from across the room, and I closed my eyes briefly. *No.* Lucas.

Luther laughed. "I was wondering how long it'd take for you to ride in on your glowing, pompously arrogant white horse."

The fallen Angel moved out from behind a tall, indoor water fountain shaped like a mermaid and hung with Mardi Gras beads, his longish, golden hair glowing as he moved. He was a tall man, built with blue eyes offset by a pair of stonewashed jeans, and a loose, untucked button-up white shirt. He was light to Luther's dark. Luther and Lucas. L&L, as I had come to dub them. So much alike in name, but so different in every other way. I had even less a history with Lucas than I did with the Demon, Luther. I'd certainly never been kissed by him.

"I feel like we're in some sort of freakish Calvin Klein photo shoot," NeeCee whispered from behind me. "I mean, seriously, I knew you had a past, but ... *wow*."

"I'm guessing you figured out the spell you did," I answered her.

She moved closer. "Yeah ..."

"Is there any way to undo it?"

NeeCee grew quiet. Quiet was never good. My attention returned to the two men dominating the room.

"This is my job, Demon," Lucas growled.

That got my attention.

"Wait," I said. I pulled away from NeeCee and moved out from behind the counter. "Job? I'm not a job."

Luther shrugged. "Maybe not before, but you are now."

His eyes were on NeeCee who was staring hard at the floor, her face red. Lucas watched the exchange curiously.

"What happened?" Lucas asked.

I looked at the fallen Angel. "My cousin and I swapped powers."

I didn't blame NeeCee for the spell. It was better to keep the focus on me. Even with my magic, she wasn't prepared for the Hounds coming to take me away, and she certainly wasn't prepared for the two men in the room with us now.

Lucas looked horrified. "Swapped?" he repeated.

Luther moved toward me, and I stepped away from him. This amused him, I could tell by the way his eyes sparkled.

"This could work to our advantage," he said, his voice low.

The sound reverberated down my spine.

"You have no place here, Demon," Lucas said hotly.

Luther ignored him. "Show me the spell you did."

He was eyeing Bernice, and I knew he was aware she had been the one to cast it. Luther was an observant man. Scarily observant.

NeeCee didn't hesitate, her shaking hands lifting the Ayers grimoire before holding it away from her.

"Page 140. It's in Latin," she warned, placing the book on the counter.

Luther took it, flipping through the pages easily before focusing on the spell NeeCee had confused with an incantation meant to reverse my connection with Demonic energy. I knew without a doubt Luther knew Latin. He knew a lot of languages.

"This is more than a complication," Luther muttered before throwing the book at Lucas.

The Angel caught it easily, skimming the page before uttering a word no Angel should be allowed to utter as he handed the book back to NeeCee. Maybe it was the whole fallen thing.

Luther was standing before me, his eyes scarlet, when the door to the back swung open.

"You're both coming with me," he said.

Chapter 4

Today, I meditated. It sounds funny, I know, but sometimes I think best when I'm still, when I close my eyes and listen. There is so much a person can hear when the eyes are gone; the wind, the trees, insects, life. I am anxious, I think, because the energy I am beginning to feel from Demons is beyond painful. I want to find a way to stop it. While meditating, I held a piece of quartz I'd used in a spell earlier in the week to help keep me focused. The corner was too sharp, and I pricked my finger while chanting a protection spell. It did something. I'm not sure what yet, but it definitely did something. I think I've found a way to help myself.

~Monroe's Totally Wicked Book of Shadows~

"What's going on?"

My aunt's voice was shrill as she and a big bosomed raven-haired beauty moved into the room. Belle, my aunt's protégé and a hopeful Pierre de Lune Coven initiate, had been with the Coven only a few months. Belle was a few years older than me, maybe 21 or 22, and she honestly reminded me of a stripper. She dressed as if she worked in Hooters for God's sake. Though, I guess I would too if I could have been their poster child. I was an easy full size B, but Belle looked surgically enhanced. Her gaze moved easily between the two men before us, and I could swear I saw her lick her lips.

Luther didn't pull any punches, winking quickly at Belle before turning to my aunt. "I'm here for your niece and your daughter."

"The hell you are," Lucas intervened.

My aunt blinked once, her face taking on an expression I knew only too well. She wasn't the head of her Coven for nothing. And she was a witch. She knew a Demon and an Angel when she saw one. It was more than obvious Luther and Lucas were *not* human.

"Care to explain?" she asked as she motioned at NeeCee.

Bernice started to move around the counter, but I grabbed her hand before she had a chance to move past. Her astonished gaze met mine. Her mother shared the same expression.

"Monroe?" Aunt Clara asked.

I avoided her gaze. "There's danger coming—" I whispered.

"And it's coming for your niece *and* your daughter," Luther finished for me.

My aunt glanced between us. "What did you do?" my aunt asked, her eyes on Bernice.

I suddenly felt defensive, pulling my cousin behind me as I faced Clara. "*We* did a spell we thought would help me. Instead, it swapped our powers. Bernice is now connected to Demonic energy, and there are Hellhounds looking for me."

Aunt Clara's face went white. Completely colorless. Belle stepped forward, moving gracefully despite her perky bosomotic (is that even a word) mother load.

"A Coven stands behind its own. We can protect them," Belle said firmly.

She looked so much like Betty Boop it wasn't even funny. I might have taken Marilyn Monroe's name, I might even dress like her the majority of the time, but I definitely lacked the curves. Belle "Betty Boop" Mason did *not* lack the curves.

Luther looked her up and down, his gaze slow. "How fast can your Coven move?" he asked, his eyes finally meeting hers.

"Excuse me?" she replied.

"If you need an explanation, then you are already too slow. There are Hellhounds being sent to take Ellie Jacobs. To Hell. And if they are not already here, they are close."

"Monroe," I corrected sullenly.

I moved between Lucas and Luther. The two of them weren't fighting anymore. At this point, collaboration was probably best.

There was a low growl outside the store, and I flinched as a foul smell permeated the shop. My aunt came unfrozen.

"The back!" she cried.

Luther shook his head. "Too late for that."

He moved toward the door, his gait calm. At the entrance, he turned, his eyes glowing red. A quick look passed between him and Lucas.

The fallen Angel grabbed Bernice and I by the arm just as Luther flung open the door. The sulfuric smell was suddenly unbearable as the Hellhounds came into view, two large dog-like creatures dominating the scene outside. I wondered briefly if they were invisible to the people on the street. This was New Orleans. The streets were rarely empty.

"Ember," I heard Luther say.

Lucas backed Bernice and I toward Aunt Clara and Belle. The two women were quiet, their eyes on the Demon's back.

"We came for the girl," the Hound in question growled.

"Well, see, that's a hard one," Luther said as he scratched his head absently. "The thing is, I have marked the girl. For now, she belongs to *me*."

A searing sensation wove its way across my lower back.

"To *us*," Lucas cut in, his jaw clenched

I grabbed my back. The pain was sharp, intense, and I didn't have my powers or an amulet to keep Luther from messing with me.

"What is it?" I whisper-yelled to Bernice as I lifted my dress up past my hips and panties. Compared to the pain, modesty could shove it! It hurt!

Bernice's eyes widened. "Um, it's a tattoo of a black serpent curled around a thorny rose."

"A freaking tattoo?" I hissed. "Seriously?"

A tramp stamp. Luther had given me a tramp stamp! The Demon was nothing if not dramatic.

A stream of smoke weaved through the room, and everyone but Luther and Lucas coughed. The smell, the density ... it was all too much.

"You play a dangerous game, Demon. You are already out of favor with our master," the Hound pointed out.

Luther grasped the door's frame, his stance comfortable. "Aw, you know me, dog. I've always had a thing for gambling."

More smoke filled the room. Luther's words were angering the creature. If someone didn't do something soon, he'd get us killed.

I started whispering under my breath, the spell's concept a simple one. Push the smoke out of the room while weaving a protection spell around the shop's exterior.

I wasn't expecting the explosion.

Chapter 5

Quartz, blood, and an incantation. It works! I wasn't sure it would at first. After all, the spell is one I created myself, but it works. Using twine, I took the spelled quartz and created an amulet. As long as it is wrapped around my neck, Demonic energy is bearable. I can still feel it, but it's bearable. I'm still not sure what it means. I still don't understand why I even feel Demons at all.

~Monroe's Totally Wicked Book of Shadows~

One moment I was standing, the next I was on my butt on the floor with my back against the wooden frame of a shattered display case while Luther knelt beside me and Lucas behind. NeeCee was sprawled on the floor still clutching the grimoire near my feet, and my Aunt Clara and Belle were leaning against the wall near the door where they had entered.

The shop's entrance was blown away, the exterior open now to the elements, and the Hellhounds were gone. Or if not gone, then hopefully knocked backwards. Luther glanced down at me, his handsome, strong face streaked with ash.

"What *was* that?" he asked.

I winced, my gaze moving from his to Bernice to my aunt. Clara was shaking her head, her eyes full of a disappointment I knew Bernice was used to. But I wasn't Bernice, and I was *not* good at being wrong, underappreciated, or condemned. I clenched my jaw.

"Um ... Did I forget to mention that NeeCee's, that's my cousin by the way, magic is *slightly* unpredictable?"

Luther choked. "Slightly?"

Okay, so he had me there. It was *way* more than slightly unpredictable. I shrugged.

"It worked though, right? I don't see any Hellhounds," I said, the hope in my voice audible.

Luther sat up, glass falling with small tinkling sounds to the hardwood floor, his expression hard.

"Witch ..." he began, his eyes meeting mine. "Do me a favor, would you?"

I nodded, my lips pressed together.

"*Don't* help," he finished.

It was more than a little humiliating, and I looked at my cousin. Did she always feel this way? Her intentions were good. I knew that. I hadn't realized how uncontrolled her magic was. Until now. I had misjudged her badly. We all had. It wasn't that her magic was inept, it was powerful. Controlling it would take a heck of a lot of practice. It made me miss my Demonic hang up.

And then I glanced back at Luther, and I suddenly didn't miss it as much.

I threw up my hands. "Fine. Suit yourself."

Belle was standing now, gaping at the damage I'd managed to do. I hated to think what would've happened had I attempted a *major* spell.

"It's going to take the whole Coven to fix this," Belle breathed.

As if I wasn't feeling bad enough.

"I'm sorry," NeeCee whispered next to me.

I glanced in her direction. She may have swapped magic with me, but if she hadn't, I never would have realized her potential. NeeCee was going to be one hell of a witch one day if she ever got over the whole *I'm not up to par* mentality. Which, in all fairness was really partly my fault too.

"Seriously, don't apologize," I answered softly. "If this wasn't Aunt Clara's shop, that would have been cool as crap."

Luther could be angry all he wanted, but truth was, I was still just a little power dizzy. I'd never had that much power at my fingertips. Or if I had, I still didn't know how to use it.

I pushed myself off the floor as sirens sounded in the distance. The Hellhounds may have been invisible to the people outside, but the explosion definitely hadn't been. A few curious onlookers cautiously approached the wreckage.

"Everyone okay in there?" a man yelled.

Luther moved to the back of the store. "We need to get out of here," he said.

No one argued. My aunt looked too shocked to do much more than shake her head. Over and over, she shook it.

"I think Bernice's magic is actually more dangerous in your hands than it ever was in hers," my aunt muttered.

My eyes narrowed. "Look ... " I began.

Luther grabbed me by the arm, pulling me behind him.

"There's no time. You and, er, Bernice?" Luther paused. "Really? *Bernice*?" he asked.

I arched a brow. "Family name," I said, my tone laced with pity.

Luther shook his head. "And I thought *my* family had issues."

Lucas snorted. "And here *I* thought *leaving* was urgent."

Luther smiled, his amusement obvious. "Right on, Glow Boy. Um ... Bernice, " Luther coughed into his hand, "and Monroe leave with us. Now."

My aunt glanced dazedly at the Demon as the sirens outside infiltrated the scene. There was no time for second thoughts. Luther had already started backing Bernice and I through the back entrance when Clara's voice rose above the chaos.

"Belle, you go with them. And remember, you represent the Coven."

This just kept getting better and better. My power had been swapped with my younger cousin whose magic was overwhelmingly unpredictable, a Demon and fallen Angel from my past were now dragging me out of a shop I had accidentally destroyed, and Betty Boop was being ordered to guard two celestial beings with motives *I* didn't even care to explore. This was going to be *so* much fun. And the only protest I could manage …

"A *tattoo*?" I asked Luther as he pulled us out into a back alley.

There was a building next door that housed a disreputable bar and grill known as McGulley's. The disreputable part wasn't because of the food, it was because the owner dabbled in prostitution. During the day, the building masqueraded as an eatery. At night, well …

"It adds character," Luther remarked.

Character, my ass!

"What are you doing?" Belle asked, and I looked up to find Luther raising a chain stretched across the back of the bar, a lock dangling from its middle.

"We need to get away, Mia Dolce. And my usual mode of transportation is a little conspicuous at the moment," Luther answered.

"Mia Dolce?" I asked.

The chain on the bar's door fell open.

"It means 'my sweet'," Lucas supplied.

If Angels were the type to roll their eyes, I think Lucas would have done so. I wasn't an Angel, I was mortal. I pretended to retch.

"This is illegal, you know," NeeCee whispered.

She sounded scared, and I reached for her hand.

The back interior of McGulley's was dark, shadows cloaking what appeared to be luxurious furniture. Several four-poster beds dominated a back wall. I felt bile rise up in my throat. So the rumors about McGulley's were true. It made me wonder why the cops hadn't ousted the operation. I suppose it depended on the bar's clientele.

"*Niiiice*," Luther drawled. Of course, he would think so.

Luther had a slight Italian accent. I knew it was because he preferred staying in Italy when he was on Earth. Maybe it was because I was American, but the way he said the word *nice* sounded clandestine. Or maybe that was just all Luther. Either way, I shivered.

We snuck through the back, being careful not to trip over items I didn't care to put a name to. I feared Bernice's innocence was getting more than a little tested, but she never said anything, although her grip on my hand tightened. It didn't loosen until Luther came to an exit leading out into another alley. This one was quieter, the sirens dulled by the sounds of pedestrians, cars, and horse drawn carriages. I had a rather belated thought concerning my aunt and insurance. Let's hope the shop was covered.

"Are we going to Italy?" I asked.

It seemed the obvious solution. S.O.S. headquarters was in Italy. My brother, Ethan, was there as well.

Luther looked over his shoulder. "No. They'll be expecting that."

"Then where?"

Lucas sidled up next to me, his arm against mine in the narrow alley. I was tall for a girl, but Luther and Lucas both towered over me by a good five inches.

"He won't expect us to stay here," Lucas said.

Luther nodded in agreement.

Belle cleared her throat. "We could go to my place. I'm fairly new to the Coven, so it might not be on the radar."

Luther smiled. "Grand idea."

I didn't think it was grand at all. Italy sounded so much more appealing than Betty Boop's house. I fervently hoped she wasn't the type to hang her bras from the shower to dry.

Belle flushed as we turned toward her, motioning to the opposite end of the alley toward a short chain link fence. "I'm two blocks that way," she said.

Luther bowed, the gesture charming. "After you."

I kept waiting for Belle to giggle, but she turned and walked away instead, her head held high. She made it to the fence and climbed it easily. How she managed with her build was beyond me, but she made it look effortless.

I scrambled over after Lucas, using his hand to help me down the opposite side. NeeCee was next, and she threw me the grimoire before climbing awkwardly, her arms shaking as she slipped.

I moved to the fence and faced her through the chain links.

"Feed off of him, NeeCee," I whispered.

I knew she felt the energy from Luther at her back. Even with the amulet exposed, she would be getting a pretty distinct hum. She had almost all modern spells memorized. With my magic, Luther's energy, and a nice incantation for agility and speed, she could accomplish a lot.

My eyes met hers, and she nodded before

murmuring under her breath. I counted to ten and knew when the look in her eyes changed and her cheeks colored that she felt the rush of magic. It wasn't overwhelming like hers. It was steady, confident. She made it over the fence faster than Belle had, leaving me gazing at Luther's dark green eyes. I handed the grimoire back to NeeCee.

"Nice, Witch. Teach her to use the dark side," Luther said.

His sarcasm irritated me.

"It's where you come from, isn't it?"

He smiled before scaling the fence, landing confidently next to me. "Yes, but I enjoy being there."

"Who doesn't?"

My question threw him and he took my elbow. Belle started moving again.

"Oh ho, Witch! Are you saying you like being bad?" Luther asked.

I ignored him, and he dropped my arm, moving back to cover the rear now that Lucas was near the front. The Angel and Demon seemed to hate each other, but they worked well together.

"Do you or Lucas have a nickname?" I asked.

Luther was quiet a moment. "Why?"

I shrugged. "Because it can get confusing after a while. You know, Lucas, Luther."

He leaned toward me. "You're asking if there's another name you can call one of us by?"

I nodded.

"Think about your back, Witch," he answered.

I glanced down at my dress, at the tattoo I knew was there. A thorny rose with a serpent wrapped around it. I shook my head.

"I don't understand."

"Thorne," he answered. "In Hell, I'm sometimes known as Thorne. You're welcome to use it, but I prefer

Luther."

I glanced up at him, my face too near his. "Why Thorne?"

He smiled, exposing sharpened teeth that visibly smoothed as I watched. "Because I look pretty, but get too close, and I bite."

I groaned. "You're full of yourself, aren't you?"

"You try living in Hell," he said. "You either grow a backbone or lose it. Literally."

And with that, *Thorne* moved past me, his eyes on Belle as she entered a small but fairly clean apartment complex near the outskirts of the French Quarter. Even as small as it was, she must pay a fortune for the place. This close to the Quarter, the rent was vicious. It's why my aunt lived above her store.

Belle climbed two flights of stairs before finally entering a landing with scarred hardwood floors. 320, 322, 324 . . . Belle paused at 326, a white door on the right side of the hall. She flashed a key, turned the knob, and entered a room decorated in scarlet. It suited Belle perfectly.

"She certainly has a thing for red," NeeCee said in my ear.

We both gaped at the stuffed red sofa sitting on a wooden floor. Beneath it was a red oval area rug. There were dark wooden end tables on
each side of the couch with lamps covered in sheer red scarves. A small, flat-screen television sat on a black, modern entertainment center next to a black chest covered in gems, red candles, and an athame. Her alter. All witches had one.

A string of red beads hung from the entrance leading into the hallway. Gaps in the beads showed a bedroom at one end and a small bathroom at the other. A small square kitchen with red appliances and only four cabinets was visible from the living area. It was a small space, but Belle was its only occupant.

"Nice taste in decor," Luther said, his voice low as he eyed the red suggestively.

Red resembled blood. It was my least favorite color. I had a thing for mixing black and white. Maybe it was my love of vintage photos and movies, or maybe I just liked the cleanliness of it. I wanted to take a dust rag after Belle's furniture, and I wasn't sure if it was because the coloring and dimness made it hard to tell if the place was dirty or because the color just made me *feel* dirty, but either way, I had the sudden urge to clean.

I looked at a clock mounted on the beige walls and noted the time, 5:15 p.m. Bernice and I had been working in the shop together around 12:00. She had cast the power swap spell around 2:00. Since then, my day had gone to hell. Literally. It wasn't NeeCee's fault. It was mine. I was the one power-tied to Demons. Even if she
hadn't done the spell, Luther would have come for me. Only now NeeCee was being dragged into it as well. I didn't count Belle. She was a big girl. But I did count the Coven, and Belle was a part of it. I was putting witches at risk.

"Coffee anyone?" Belle asked as she moved toward her kitchen.

Only NeeCee and Lucas answered in the affirmative. I think NeeCee just wanted something to do with her hands. Lucas wanted two tablespoons of sugar. Angels had a thing for sugar when on Earth. I had learned that from Dayton. I missed her.

"Greece," I mumbled.

Luther "Thorne" looked at me askance, his brow furrowed. I shook my head. It was confusing calling him Luther with Lucas present, but I preferred it, too. I'd never known him as Thorne, but now knowing he had an alter ego made him even more interesting. Two names. One man.

"What?" he asked.

I blushed, which is not like me at all, but I hadn't meant to say Greece out loud.

"It's a game I play," I muttered.

Luther raised a brow. "A game?"

"When I don't like where I am, I imagine myself somewhere else."

Luther looked away. It was *my* game. He didn't have to like it. I was doing a darn good job visualizing the beaches and white stone buildings of Greece, the breeze off the Mediterranean, and the ruins. It was better than a room dominated by red.

Belle walked back into the living area with two red, stone mugs.

"What now?" she asked.

Luther and Lucas' gaze met. "We wait for Monroe's magic to return," the Angel answered. "Until then, we find a way to rid her of her connection to the underworld."

Belle leaned against a bar stool cushioned in red.

"It's hard for the Coven to understand Monroe's connection with Demons. Wicca is a belief centered on the Earth, the Goddess, and her Consort. Our individual practices differ, but it all narrows down to that."

NeeCee, who had been clutching the Ayers grimoire, placed it on one of Belle's end tables so she could grip her coffee with both hands.

Luther watched Belle. "Hard to understand or not, Hell exists, and it wants Monroe. Or better yet, her magic. It's rare for a mortal to be born connected to the underworld. *Unless* they have Demon blood."

Belle looked at me, her eyes wide. "Could it be?" she asked.

I shook my head. "No. No way! *Not* possible."

Luther shrugged. "Maybe not, but it may be time to trace that family history of yours. Start at the beginning."

His gaze moved to the grimoire. Mine followed, a strange fluttery sensation in the pit of my stomach. Could there be Demon blood in my family?

"There's no way," NeeCee interjected. "I mean, if there was Demon blood in our family, why only Monroe?"

Luther glanced at me. "Good question."

Chapter 6

Demonic energy makes my power stronger. Anytime I perform a spell anywhere near a Demon, it magnifies its power. This should scare me. Really, it should. And truth be told, it does.

~Monroe's Totally Wicked Book of Shadows~

One day. Only *one* day, and I was standing in the middle of a red room with a big bosomed, raven-haired witch, my wide-eyed cousin, a fallen Angel, and a Demon while questioning my lineage. My existence.

I moved to the grimoire and lifted it. "How do I get my magic back?"

Luther moved to my side, his hand skimming the grimoire's worn leather cover. A Pentacle design was etched on the top. His fingers brushed mine, and I pulled away.

"The spell Bernice did is temporary. How temporary is unknown. Your magic will return on its own," Luther said.

He took the grimoire from me, pulling it from my grasp as if he had every right to the contents. And I let him have it. I offered no resistance because, right now, he and Lucas knew way more than the rest of us.

He flipped the cover open, scanning the date on the first page, his eyes dark.

"The beginning of the grimoire is illegible," I said quietly.

Luther's eyes met mine. "If only you knew how old I were, Witch. Your grimoire begins in the 12th Century, in 1141 to be exact.

"And this matters because?" Belle asked.

Lucas watched Luther's face, his eyes narrowed. "You really think following a book will save her?"

Luther glared at the fallen Angel. "Stay out of my head, Angel. I didn't invite you in."

I stared at them, my eyes wide. "What do you mean follow a book?"

"It means he thinks we should trace your ancestry. Follow the grimoire from its beginning to where your curse begins," Lucas explained.

"My curse?" I repeated dumbly.

Luther looked up at me, his face grave. "To an Angel, being linked to Demons is a curse. Consider yourself blighted."

Well, that was comforting.

"And so we trace my ancestry?" I asked.

Lucas nodded. "That's the idea. A history lesson while chased by the denizens of Hell. The Demon is insane."

Luther looked at him. "You have a better idea, White Knight?"

Lucas frowned. NeeCee had long since laid her coffee down, her face full of terror. Belle was standing now, her own eyes narrowed.

"You want to trot all over the world trying to find a link with Demons that may not exist?" she asked.

Luther smiled at her, his gaze full of sexual interest. It made her squirm, which was more than likely his intention.

"Theoretically. It's a much better plan than feeding her frog parts and trying white and grey magic that has no effect on Demonic power," Luther stated.

Belle's mouth dropped open. "Are you suggesting black magic then?"

Luther's expression grew hard. "I'm suggesting we find out where the Ayers messed up. Or find out if they did anything that may have tied Monroe to the underworld. You can leave the black magic up to me. No worries, sweetheart, my soul is already corrupted."

Fear finally crossed Belle's features. If she hadn't known how dangerous Luther "Thorne" Craig was, she did now.

Luther moved away then, putting distance between himself and the others. I followed, looking up into his face as he stared out of a window at the darkening, busy street.

"Why are you really doing this?" I asked.

He looked down at me. "Because my brother is bound to your best friend, and he asked me to. One favor. It's all I'm willing to give even him."

"So I'm a favor?"

He looked away. "I don't save people, I destroy them. Yes, you're a favor. I like who I am. I have no problem being the Demon I was born to be. I believe in my brother's cause, giving hybrids like us a choice. My choice is Hell. That will never change. I like the dark."

Luther's brother, Marcas, was a hybrid Demon, a ruler in the Outer Levels of Hell. He was also a champion for half-breed Demons because he gave them a choice. Hell or Exile. Like Exiled Angels who live outside Heaven, they could choose to live outside Hell's rule. I guess I respected that.

"I'm okay being a favor. I think," I said, my nose scrunched.

Luther looked down at me. "Then the journey begins, Witch. We find out where your people screwed up."

That was it then. I looked at the clock on the wall. 6:00. In 6 hours, I had someone else's powers, I was a Demon's favor, and I was about to trace my family's lineage on a large scale.

Luther held his hand up in the air, and red elongated candy magically materialized in his palm. The symbolism wasn't lost on me.

"Hot tamale?" he asked, amused.

I thought of the black candle NeeCee had lit before the spell. 6 black wax spots. 6 hours. 6 p.m. A Demon sometimes known as Thorne.

I was screwed.

Chapter 7

I think Dayton is in love with Marcas. In a way, I don't blame her. There is something about the Demon. He seems completely emotionless, but I wonder if that's because of who he is. He's been around for a long, long time. And now, when its time for them to become unbound, I feel reluctance from them both. We fought Lucifer's army in Petra. It was the scariest thing I have ever had to do. Satan tried to possess Luther, tried to use him to fight his own brother, but he was wearing an amulet he took from me, and it worked! It kept Lucifer from possessing him. What does this all mean?

~Monroe's Totally Wicked Book of Shadows~

The Ayers' grimoire looked eerie where it sat on Belle's end table, the brown leather cracked in places, the pages yellowed but protected by magic. It was old magic. Ancient magic.

The book had always fascinated me as a child during the odd times when my mother would let me sit in on circles, my eyes moving to the old text. So much magic, so many Ayers witches.

"Demons in our family," Bernice whispered.

I looked over my shoulder to find her eyes wide, her fear much more pronounced than mine.

"Hush, NeeCee. We don't know that," I said.

My eyes went back to the book. It was late now.

Luther was in the kitchen, deep in some debate with Belle about our family grimoire and a wild goose chase. Lucas had left earlier, only to return with some of mine and NeeCee's things. NeeCee had eyed the pink duffel bag Lucas had brought back with longing. I could see the question she refused to ask on her face. Bernice missed her mother.

Unlike NeeCee, I was used to being alone. I had an amazing family. My mother and father had raised my brothers and I with a kind but firm hand, guiding us when they needed to, but never sheltering us. There *had* been some secrets, don't get me wrong. I hadn't found out about my father's role in the S.O.S. until I was seventeen, but I didn't blame them for that. All in all, they had raised us the best they could, and then trusted us to make the right decisions.

For a while, I had chosen to work with the Swords of Solomon like my father and my oldest brother, Ethan. But my powers began to bother me more and more, the Demons the S.O.S. often came in contact with causing me pain even with the amulet, and so I had made the decision to seek out the Coven. When I had called my mother, she'd agreed with me. She was as worried as I was about my connection to Demons, and although I fought often with my Aunt Clara on how to approach my so-called curse, I was willing to try most anything. Until now.

I leaned over and picked up the black backpack Lucas had laid at my feet. It was old and worn with a faded scene from the *Wizard of Oz* imprinted along the front.

Unzipping it, I sighed in relief when I saw my own clothes inside.

I looked up at Belle. "Mind if I change?" I asked, gesturing at the small bathroom just beyond the red beaded curtain. She looked over at me and nodded.

"Quickly," Luther insisted, his dark eyes on my face. "We shouldn't stay here long."

I heeded his warning, moving into the too small restroom just long enough to use the facility, rinse off, and shirk the dress and platforms I'd worn all day. I pulled out a pair of dark blue skinny jeans, and an oversized navy t-shirt with the words *Wanted Dead or Alive* along the front and cringed. First off, Lucas had a messed up sense of humor. Secondly, he definitely believed in comfort over beauty.

I stepped into the jeans and tied the too long shirt off with a ponytail holder before digging a pair of flat, black slouch boots out of the bag. The boots made me grin. The fallen angel had probably been looking for tennis shoes. If it had been Dayton, he would have had no problem. Me? Nope, I didn't do tennis shoes. He was lucky I owned anything without a heel.

I straightened and looked in the mirror. What little makeup I had attempted that morning had worn off, and there were shadows under my eyes, my skin too pale to hide the weariness.

I pulled the headband out of my white blonde hair and threw it into the backpack. My hair was straight and too fine to wear long. I kept it bobbed just below my chin. It swung there now, slanted bangs falling into my face.

My blue eyes met my reflection in the mirror, the sight distorted briefly when I leaned over to splash cold water into my face. And then there they were again. The same blue eyes. No different. No less tired. No less confused.

"Here goes nothing," I murmured.

The moment in the bathroom was more about bolstering my courage than changing clothes, and I stood up straight, my shoulders back before grabbing the backpack and moving out of the room.

Belle, Luther, and Lucas were standing around the grimoire, the book open, when I reappeared. NeeCee stood behind them ringing her hands until she heard the red beads swing against the wall as I entered.

Luther looked up, his eyes cutting to Lucas when he caught a glimpse of the t-shirt I wore.

"Really?" Luther asked.

A corner of Lucas' lips twitched, but he managed to fight the grin.

I pointed at the book. "What are you doing?"

I dropped the backpack on the couch as I knelt in front of the grimoire.

Luther peered down at me from where he stood on the opposite side of the table. "How much of this book can your family actually read?" he asked me.

The insulting tone he used made me tense, and I stuck the end of my tongue between my teeth as I stared down at the grimoire. It was open to the first few pages, the words scrawled within foreign to me.

"We've had some of it translated," I said defensively.

Belle swept her hand over the text. "And what hasn't been translated, Clara was looking into. You aren't the first person to believe the answers to Monroe's problem might be in the book."

I clenched my jaw. I really hated it when people referred to me as a problem. I let my eyes move up to Luther's. His gaze met mine and held it.

NeeCee made an uncomfortable gasping sound, and I saw her rub her arms from the corner of my eye. I wished there was something I could do to shield her from Luther's energy, but he already wore an amulet.

"I'm assuming you can read it," I pointed out. "So does it really matter what we haven't translated?"

Luther didn't comment. He looked at Belle, which honestly bothered me more than getting no reply. "The first entry is from a young girl. Eta. No last name. It seems to be a running theme in this book," he said.

NeeCee moved behind me before sitting on the couch, her leg touching my back. She was shivering.

"There would be no need right? Wouldn't they have all been Ayers?" NeeCee asked.

Luther shook his head. "Maybe. If all of the females in the line kept their maiden name. But some of them must have married, and the ones who did would have taken their husbands' names." Luther turned a few pages, his forehead creased. "Did Eta marry an Ayers or was it her father's name?"

I looked up at him, an image playing behind my eyes.

"It was her father," I whispered. It seemed NeeCee hadn't acquired all of my powers. Either that or we shared a similar talent. It seemed more likely than the power swap spell fading. Even weak spells lasted longer than a day. "Her father was an Ayers," I repeated loudly, my tone sure.

Luther's eyes swung to mine. His gaze was like a knife. Even when he wasn't trying to, his eyes cut too deep.

"Touch the book," he ordered.

I felt strangely compelled to follow his command, but I fought it, standing so that I was no longer kneeling before him, my jaw hard. "What?"

Luther's gaze moved between Bernice and I. "Did you finish the power swap spell you did in the shop?" he asked NeeCee.

She swallowed hard. "Most of it. Monroe stopped me before I read the final line."

Luther's eyes were on mine again. "That's not good news for you."

I stared at him. "Why?"

Belle placed a hand on the table next to the

grimoire. "It's not good because the spell wasn't finalized. It means Bernice gave you her magic, but all of yours wasn't transferred to her. Just the curse."

"Wonderful," NeeCee mumbled.

I glared down at her. "Don't you start mocking the curse too. It's your fault you carry it now. Not mine."

NeeCee looked away from me, her cheeks pink, and I felt immediately bad about my sharp tone.

Lucas moved behind Luther. "It could be good too," the fallen Angel said. "A power swap spell can last a month when finished. This way, it could fade in days."

Belle placed her hands firmly on her hips. "What would either of you know about witchcraft?"

Luther laughed, the sound harsh, cold. His eyes were red when they met Belle's. "Witch, we've been around long before your people's first sacred circle."

There was something in his tone, something dark and angry. Belle stepped back, her movement bringing her closer to Lucas, but the fallen Angel looked away from her. Whatever memory Belle had brought up, the Demon and fallen Angel shared.

Luther's eyes came back to mine. "Touch the book, Monroe."

Something about the set of his lips made me obey, my eyes on his face rather than the grimoire. I didn't want to touch the book. I wanted to touch him. Without the electrical tingle my curse usually made me feel, I couldn't
help but wonder what my clairvoyant powers could discover about him.

The pads of my fingers landed gently against the old paper, the tickling sensation not unusual. I had touched the pages many times before, and nothing had happened. But now, I wasn't being held back by the curse.

One moment I was standing in Belle's living room,

the next I was somewhere dark and cold.

My eyes went wide.

"Monroe," I heard someone call, the voice distant. It was Belle.

"Shut up, Witch," Luther admonished.

His voice, too, was distant. I was on the edge of a forest. It was night, and there was a full moon in the sky, the silvery light making frosty leaves and grass glow. My t-shirt and jeans were suddenly not enough, and I wrapped an arm around my middle, my teeth chattering. I knew I was in a vision. I'd had them too often not to realize what was happening.

I could still hear Belle arguing with Luther somewhere beyond the vision's veil, but I also knew better than to speak. Magic, especially old magic was tricky. If the grimoire's protection spell warded against visionaries, speaking could destroy me.

My eyes skirted the forest, traveling over the dark, spindly trees, their limbs bare of leaves. An owl hooted, and branches swayed eerily in the breeze, but I wasn't afraid. Witches embraced
the night. We held many circles in dark forests and fields. It put us closer to nature, to the world as it should be.

I exhaled, and gazed in fascination at the way my breath misted out in front of me. There were exclamations from afar. They weren't part of the vision, and I ignored them. Where my mind was, so was my body. My breath would be as visible to the people in Belle's living room as it was to me.

A voice, a clear feminine voice, rang through the clearing before a cloaked figure suddenly brushed past me, long silvery white blonde hair flying back into my face. She smelled like roses, and she was laughing. I blinked, fighting not to stumble. I knew if I did, my hand would come off of the grimoire. The book was the only thing keeping me here.

The girl called out to someone, her language foreign to me. Other voices answered hers. I could see smoke now coming from small fires lit beside a lake. The full moon glistened on the water, the reflection wavering with the movement of the waves. There were brown hooded figures everywhere. Two white cloaks stood out among the rest.

Small stones circled the fires, and there were cows amidst the group of people, some of them being led around the flames. It hit me then. It was cold. Winter was approaching, and these people were cleansing their cattle using the
power of the smoke. Samhain. These people, *my* people, were celebrating Samhain.

The blonde-haired girl laughed again, pulling up her hood as she met with one of the white-cloaked figures, her hands clasped in his. Words were spoken between them, and still I couldn't comprehend the language. I narrowed my eyes, my ears straining.

The girl spoke again, and this time the language was clear. I thanked the Goddess for the ability to understand.

"Father," she said, her voice light.

The white-cloaked man looked up, his shadowed gaze on the forest. I could just make out his pale skin beneath the fire lit hood.

"You were not followed?" he asked. She shook her head. "Good," he responded, "Let's proceed."

The people had begun to gather, circling the fires, their chants soothing, when I heard the men in the forest behind me.

"Stay low, boy!" a man hissed. I stiffened. "You are young yet, but you will understand one day," the man continued. "They are witches. Their humanity stolen by magic. It is our job to kill them."

My heart began to beat wildly. Hunters. I would know them anywhere. I had cut my teeth on Hunter stories. I wanted to warn the people in the clearing, but it would do no good. The vision was of the past. It would make no
difference, and speaking while in a vision could hurt only me.

I closed my eyes and exhaled again before reopening my lids.

In a single blink, the scene had changed. Screaming. There was screaming everywhere. And blood. An arrow protruded from the chest of one of the white-cloaked figures, the crimson stain around it stark against the light fabric. It was the girl's father.

"Go," I heard him gurgle. "Find Mac. Go with him. He will keep you safe. Run, Eta. Run."

The girl clamped her hands over her mouth to keep from crying out as her father crumpled to the ground. Her hood had fallen back, her hair making her a visible target, and she tugged it on again, falling to the ground and crawling as figures around her ran in varying directions. It was enough to shield her, and she slunk into the forest.

I looked up, my face coming nose to nose with a Hunter. The man was tall and broad, his face covered in red facial hair, parts of it braided. His eyes gleamed, the black depths ominous. Blood speckled his face. His breath smelled like some type of liquor, and his cheeks were flushed.

I broke two rules then. I gasped, the noise loud in the vision, and I talked directly to the apparition.

"No," I whispered.

It wasn't the first time I'd ever spoken in a vision. The last time, I'd been violently ill for two days afterwards, but it was the first time an apparition ever looked at me. And *not* just looked at me, but *saw* me. The Hunter's eyes widened, his breath quickening as he raised his hand. He gripped a dagger, the metal gleaming in the moonlight. His eyes narrowed on mine, and he grinned.

I froze, shock gluing me to the spot, my horrified eyes on the blade. No. It wasn't possible.

The blade lowered.

Something slammed into me, and the vision by the lake was gone, the Hunter's gleeful eyes burned into my brain.

Chapter 8

I talked to my mother about my powers today. Up until now, I'd kept the Demonic stuff from her. The look on her face made me wish I'd not said anything. There was terror in her eyes. Terror and confusion. I'm pretty positive her gaze mirrored my own. I've made the decision to work with the Swords of Solomon in Italy for a while. Mom is returning to the States. She is going to gather the Coven in an attempt to discover what may be causing my connection with Demons.

~Monroe's Totally Wicked Book of Shadows~

"Are you stupid?"

Luther's angry voice penetrated my foggy head, and I shook off the vision. I was in Belle's living room again, my back on the floor and Luther was straddling me, his hand just beneath my chin.

"He saw me," I whispered, my eyes coming up to meet the Demon on top of me. His free hand was on the floor next to my head, and I could see the muscles rippling in his arm just under the sleeve of his black t-shirt. I didn't remember him removing his leather trench coat.

"You never speak during a vision," Luther hissed, his face lowering so that his nose was nearly touching mine, his breath on my face.

I didn't argue with him. I knew speaking

during a vision was dangerous. Question was, how did he?

My eyes searched his. "He saw me," I repeated.

A shadow fell over us, blue jean-clad legs just visible beyond Luther's arm.

"Enough, Demon. You can get off of her now," Lucas demanded.

Luther's eyes remained on mine a moment longer before he glanced upward, one corner of his lip curling as he sat up, his hands lifted. The weight of his hips was heavier against mine, and my cheeks flamed.

"Getting up," Luther conceded, his grin growing as he realized my discomfort.

If I was being honest, it was more than that. There had always been something about Luther Craig that made my blood boil, made parts of my body I wanted to ignore heat up. And he knew it. I wanted to blame it on my Demonic connection, but now that I was temporarily without it, I had to admit it wasn't.

Luther's weight was gone as abruptly as it had arrived, and Lucas' outstretched hand replaced it. I took it, allowing the Angel to help me up before running my clammy hands down the sides of my pants, my eyes meeting the shocked expressions on Belle and NeeCee's faces.

"What the hell was that?" Belle asked.

I shook my head, my gaze going back to Luther. He was in front of me, his stance casual, his face unreadable.

"There was a Hunter in the vision. He saw me," I said a third time.

"What did you think would happen?" Lucas asked. "You spoke in a vision, Monroe. Something bad was bound to happen."

My angry gaze swept the blond Angel before moving back to Luther. "Not that! Never! *That* should never have happened. An apparition should not have been able to see me. It's the past. I was only a spectator there. An *invisible* visitor. I should not have been seen."

"And yet," Luther said calmly, "with NeeCee's added powers it was possible. Seems there is more than one secret in your family."

I stepped toward him. He didn't back away. "What?" I asked. "What are you talking about?"

Luther's gaze went to Belle's. "How long have Hunters been after Bernice?" he asked suddenly.

NeeCee gasped, and I stiffened. *What the hell?*

"Hunters after NeeCee?" I breathed.

I took another step forward. It brought me next to Luther, and my shoulder brushed his arm as my gaze went to Belle.

The raven-haired witch was fiddling with the corner of a page in the grimoire, her eyes looking anywhere but at us.

"Belle?" NeeCee asked, her voice small. She sounded so young, even at sixteen, and anger coursed through my veins.

"You aren't the only cursed Ayers, Monroe," Belle muttered.

The sound that came out of NeeCee's mouth sounded mysteriously close to a sob. She was used to being a disappointment, a klutz, and an all around disaster. But a curse? I personally thought the other stuff was hella bad, but by the look on NeeCee's face, I guess being cursed was worse. Go figure.

"What do you mean?" I asked,

Belle looked up then, her gaze going to NeeCee. "For centuries, there has always been one Ayers witch who was different. Something about her power draws Hunters ..."

NeeCee's sobs broke into Belle's words. I didn't move, and Belle's gaze moved to mine.

"Because of this, many of the Ayers witches in the past with this *calling* power were abandoned, left to live alone until Hunters finally destroyed them. Bernice was born with this power."

I simply stared.

Wow. Ayers witches. One cursed with ties to Demons. Another born with powers that called to killers. All in one line of witches. What the hell had we done to deserve it? And why did Belle know about it while NeeCee and I didn't?

"Why weren't we told?" I asked.

Belle's face fell. "Because even the coven doesn't understand it. Including your mother and Clara. There has been talk of other Ayers witches born with Bernice's power, rumors of others with the same Demonic abilities as yours, but no one seems to remember why. And no one has been able to translate the book. The language is odd. Your vision is the first real look at that part of the book."

I was confused. "The language they spoke in the vision didn't seem all that strange. Just foreign. And there's no one who could translate it?"

"The words in the book are Demonic, written in a language only Demons use," Luther said suddenly.

I froze, my eyes going to his. "Demonic?" I shivered. "Seriously?"

"Oh, my God," NeeCee breathed.

I leaned in closer to Luther. "Then why don't you read it?" I asked. "You're a Demon."

I was trying everything in my power not to panic. There were Demonic words in my family's grimoire!

Luther's return gaze was hard, unrelenting. "There is no single Demon language. When it is written, it is only translatable by the person who wrote it, and it changes often. The only person who can translate it is someone directly tied to the person who wrote it."

What he left unsaid was more powerful than his words.

"Roe—" NeeCee began.

I didn't let her finish. I'd had a vision about a part of our family's grimoire written in a language that could only be interpreted by someone directly linked to the author. What that meant for me ... I was scared. Scared made me angry, and I turned to Belle, my eyes burning.

"What was the Coven going to do?" I asked. "Just wait until Hunters showed up at the shop to kill Bernice and then take a stand against them?"

Belle's jaw tightened, her eyes full of sympathy. "We were working on it."

I threw up my hands. "Like you were working on my curse too, right?" My gaze moved to Luther's profile. "You got any bright ideas, Demon? Cause I'm all out of 'em."

Luther glanced down at me before looking over at Lucas. "Can you feel them?" Luther asked.

Lucas nodded. "There are hellhounds near."

Oh, wonderful! Hunters and Hellhounds. Life was simply rose-colored at the moment.

I grabbed my backpack and lifted the grimoire, placing it inside before anyone had a chance to tell me not to. NeeCee slung her duffel bag over her shoulder, her face red and her nose swollen. I wanted to comfort her, but there was no time.

"As for my bright idea, Monroe," Luther added. "I suggest we find some Witch Hunters."

I froze. I hadn't expected that. "We *what*?" I asked dumbly.

Luther shrugged. "There may be a closer connection between you and Bernice than you know. Somewhere in your family's history, two witches in your line were cursed, one to death, the other to the devil. Why sit around waiting to be hunted when we can be the hunter?"

Lucas groaned. "Right up your alley. Right, Demon?"

Luther looked at the Angel and grinned. It was a feral smile, his eyes red. There was something dangerous about Luther. Something that spoke of dark corners, blood, and death.

"Where to?" Belle asked, her voice strained. She wasn't fighting Luther's crazy idea. By the dark look in her eyes, I wondered if it was out of fear or disgust.

Luther didn't break eye contact with the Angel. "To Scotland. There are bound to be Ayers witches still there, and I think this all began with Eta."

So the Eta from the grimoire was from Scotland?

Lucas didn't argue. He walked to the apartment window instead and opened it. "Any truth to the whole witches can fly myth?" he asked.

It was dark outside, the red curtains around the open window blowing into the room. The night smelled like wet cement and old beignets.

"If you mean broomsticks, then no," I said before Belle could answer. "There are certain spells, but I don't know them, and I don't trust NeeCee's powers."

Lucas looked at Belle. "And you?" he asked.

The dark-haired witch nodded. "I'm not a blood witch, but Clara has designed a few spells that gives me many of the same powers when needed."

It irked me that she could fly. It irked me even more that my aunt was the reason she could. Something about the idea that Belle could do anything better than me *really* rubbed me wrong.

"Then I'll take Monroe," Luther said quickly, his eyes on Lucas. "You take Bernice." The Angel's return gaze was stormy.

NeeCee took a deep breath. "We're going to fly?"

she asked, her small voice quivering. She was only two years younger than me, and yet I felt so much older.

"We fly," Luther answered.

And with that, I was suddenly wrapped in his arms and airborne before I even had a chance to breath. Somewhere behind us, I heard NeeCee shriek and Belle mutter something in Latin too low for me to understand. And then there was the smell of sulfur.

Luther had been right. The Hellhounds were still nearby, and yet they hadn't come to find me again. Why? Were they biding their time? And why would they do that? Because Luther had put a serpent wrapped rose on my back? That seemed kind of lame.

My fingers went to Luther's where he held me around the waist, and I gripped his hands. This wasn't my first time flying. I'd done it before in the past with one of my closest friends, Conor Reinhardt, who was also a gargoyle. But Conor wasn't Luther. Conor didn't make my stomach feel like an utter mess.

"The hounds are near." I searched the skies. "I know Hellhounds. Why don't they take me now?" I asked the Demon in the darkness.

His hands tightened on my waist. "Because I made you mine," he whispered against my ear.

I shivered. "Yours?"

He chuckled. "You don't feel me inside of your head, Monroe? I'm a Demon, and your powers have been swapped with your cousin's. You have no protection."

My fingernails were suddenly digging into his flesh. He wouldn't dare. He wouldn't!

"What have you done?" I whispered.

"Lift your hand," Luther ordered.

One of my hands rose into the air. I tried to lower it, but it wouldn't budge. I groaned with the effort. Still nothing.

"Now relax," Luther said.

My hand went limp, moving back to his at my waist.

The Demon's lips brushed my ear. "Possession, my dear witch, can be such a beautiful thing."

Chapter 9

I stood on one of the balconies at S.O.S. headquarters this afternoon, my eyes on the vineyard just beyond the property, and I made my decision. I don't want to leave Italy. I don't want to leave Dayton and Conor when things are just beginning to come together for them, but my powers are overwhelming me. I am having strange visions. Sometimes, I see myself doing bad things in them. Have I become so connected to Demons that their evil is corrupting me? Or are the visions of the future?

~Monroe's Totally Wicked Book of Shadows~

I fell limp in Luther's arms, my head spinning. *Possessed.*

"You asshole," I breathed.

He chuckled. "Tsk, tsk, Witch. If you're anything like your friend Dayton, then possessing you is going to make my job a whole lot easier."

I grit my teeth. "You really think so?" I asked.

"I'm banking on it."

I looked up at him. "Stay out of my head, Luther Craig."

His eyes met mine, and the twinkle in their depths was obvious. "Which part? Your childhood, the present, or your thoughts?"

I struggled in his arms.

"You don't think I'd let you go?" Luther asked. "Try me."

I still struggled. "How *dare* you! My thoughts, my head, are mine. Mine! Everyone should have that. *No one* should lose their free will, you understand me?" I took a deep breath. "Is that what the stupid tattoo is for? For possession?"

Luther chuckled. "The tattoo is gone, Monroe. You'd know that if you had looked for it in the mirror earlier. It wasn't even necessary and has nothing to do with possession."

I fumed. It was for what then? Fun?

"You have one twisted sense of humor!" I exclaimed, kicking him firmly in the shin with my heel.

Luther didn't seem the least bit fazed. I stopped struggling. We were attracting attention. I could see Lucas holding Bernice in front of us, and Belle was beside them, her body surrounded by a blue glow. Somewhere during the struggle, Luther and I had fallen back.

"Everything okay?" Lucas asked.

The Angel's eyes met mine, and I looked away. "I'm fine," I answered.

There was silence, and I could feel Luther's chin resting on my shoulder, his breath against the sensitive skin just below my ear.

"The Angel doesn't know?" I whispered.

"Funny isn't it?" Luther asked, his amusement obvious. "I've learned to hide a lot of things over the years."

I inhaled slowly. "I'm not Dayton."

Luther's hair tickled my cheek. I tried to ignore how intimate it felt, but couldn't.

"No," he conceded. "You're not."

I swallowed hard. I wanted to imagine myself

somewhere else, but no matter how vivid my imagination, nothing could compare to being here right now.

"Nice to know you think so," Luther murmured.

I cursed him in my head, and he laughed.

"Why are you doing this?" I asked. "Do you fear being out of control?"

"Not as much as you do," Luther answered.

I tensed because I knew he was right. I was a control freak and obsessive compulsive. It was the reason why I carried dozens of those little bottles of hand sanitizer and a really thick day planner.

"It's *my* mind," I finally stated.

Luther lifted his head. "For now, it's *ours*. I'm strong, Monroe. I'm not saying that to be arrogant, I'm saying it because it's true. If anyone can take a stand against Lucifer, it's the sons and daughters of Cain and Lilith. It's why Marcas sent me. If you think I'm bad, you don't want to be controlled by the worst Demon of us all."

I glanced up at him. "Are you saying if you didn't possess me, then Lucifer would? You're wrong. I could make an amulet."

Luther grew quiet and then, "You can't make one now after the power swap spell, and I won't give up the one you gave me. In the long run, it's safer for me to wear the amulet while I possess you."

I didn't say anything else. He was right. I hated it, but there it was. In the past, I'd seen the amulet protect Luther from being possessed by Lucifer. He needed it more than I did right now because he was stronger than me.

"You can't be all bad, Luther," I said.

His head lowered again. Something about the Demon touched my heart. I'm not sure why. I didn't know him at all. All I knew about him was his parentage, his brother, and a kiss he'd given me once.

"I have never pretended to be," Luther said. "But I also don't pretend to be something I'm not. Sometimes being bad is better. It makes it easier to slay the monsters."

Some things can be said about being held close by a person when you barely know them. For one, it forces you to ask questions you never would have asked before, to make conversation when it might be better to remain silent.

"I don't think of myself as cursed," I said quietly. Luther tensed, but I didn't give him a chance to speak. "I've known for a little while now that I am connected somehow to Hell and to Demons. It scared me. I had even quit sleeping at night, as if the dark somehow made things worse, but there is also something I've learned from it."

"You realize," Luther interrupted, "that you don't have to say anything. I already know what you're thinking."

I snorted. "You do realize that saying things out loud makes them more real than thinking them, right?"

Luther remained silent, and I laughed. "You *do* realize it, don't you? Ha! That's why you don't want me to talk. Fine, so I'm a control freak, but you fear what exactly? Reality?"

He didn't answer, and I laid my head back on his shoulder so that I could look up into his face. His lips were tight, his skin pale in the darkness. It was an illusion. Luther had olive skin.

"I've learned," I continued, "that being damned is the saddest, most loneliest feeling in the world. I think the pain I feel from Demons like you isn't anger, it's fear. It's a constant search for something real. Freedom from pain, death, and persecution."

"You don't know what you're talking about," Luther

huffed.

I snorted again. "Don't I?"

His eyes moved down to mine, and our gazes caught.

"I told you before I'm not Dayton," I said. "And you, Luther, are no Marcas. You let yourself feel more than he does. Quit pretending you don't."

"You need a restraining order on your mouth," Luther growled.

I smiled. "Why? You're already in my head, right? You're the one who removed the barriers, Demon. There are no holds barred now."

He looked away from me, his eyes moving to the sky above. The wind blew my hair against my face, the chill refreshing. It was January, and where ever we were, it wasn't Louisiana anymore. It was too cold.

Luther's arms wrapped themselves more securely around me, his body shielding mine from the elements. His skin heated, and I grew drowsy. This day had been too long, and full of too many revelations. I was a cursed witch wanted by Lucifer, and Bernice was a cursed witch who was a natural magical beacon for Hunters, a witch's most fearsome enemy.

I shouldn't want to sleep, and yet here I was in Luther's arms, the cold wind brushing my cheeks and tangling my hair, and that's exactly what I did.

Chapter 10

New Orleans, Louisiana. It's a place where it's okay to be different. Not just outwardly, but inwardly too. It's why I came here. My Aunt Clara lives here, along with her branch of the Ayers Coven. The Moonstone Coven, or whatever else it is Clara calls it in French. I like Moonstone better. Either way, Clara has welcomed me into her home, and we've discussed my powers. The visions are normal. It's my Ayers gift. But the Demonic stuff isn't. I think I scare people. Sometimes, I scare myself.

~Monroe's Totally Wicked Book of Shadows~

When I woke, we were in a small, one-room cabin, and I was in a bed with several quilted blankets over me. I was warm and reluctant to move, my eyes skirting the room's wooden interior. There was a rusted wooden stove in the corner with a twisted pipe that exited through the roof, and another bed opposite mine. It was iron, and I could just make out Bernice's shape on the thin mattress beneath another set of faded quilts.

I sat up.

Shadows moved along the walls, created by the flames inside the stove's open door, and the cabin's floor was littered with twigs and dead leaves. Wind raked my face, bringing my attention to the cabin's cracked doorway. There was light beyond the crack, but it was dull. The moon? Or dawn?

I threw my covers back, my hands going instantly to my bare arms as goose bumps popped up along my skin. The room was crazy cold even with the stove burning, and I looked hastily for my missing boots and backpack as I stepped onto the wooden planks below. My royal blue, manicured toenails peeked up at me, the only real splash of color in a grey, cold world.

"Monroe," a voice whispered, and I placed a finger against my lips.

"Shhhhhhh," I hissed.

NeeCee was sitting up in her own bed now, her eyes wide and scared behind crooked glasses.

"Where are we?" NeeCee asked.

I located my boots and slipped them on. They weren't much protection against the cold, but they made me feel better. Something about having shoes on made me feel less vulnerable. My backpack was against the cabin wall, and I lifted it.

"I don't know," I answered while pulling one of the quilts off of the bed and wrapping it around my shoulders. "Come on, NeeCee. Find your shoes."

She did as ordered, and I crept over to the door. The crack didn't afford much of a view, but I recognized the location instantly, and I
yanked on the door.

"What are you doing?" NeeCee asked horrified.

I tugged harder. The hinges were so old, they groaned, and NeeCee stumbled up behind me.

"Stop, Monroe! We don't know where we are! They could have left us here to die for all we know. Think about it. It seems reasonable. What better way to get rid of two cursed witches than together?"

I huffed. "I mean too much to them for them to kill me."

NeeCee coughed. "Arrogant much?"

The anger in her tone was refreshing, and I grinned. It was nice to hear her do something other than shiver.

"No, truth," I pointed out. "Hell wants me. If Luther and Lucas abandon me, then it leaves me open for possession, and they don't want that."

NeeCee grew silent for only a moment before she leaned in to help me pull on the door. Between the two of us, we managed to get it open just enough we could slide through.

There was a hop down from there, the wooden steps that once sat in front of the door now rotted away, and we landed in snow. A small wooden house sat to the side of the yard, and I scrunched my nose.

"They couldn't find somewhere more technologically advanced? A real toilet would have been nice," I complained.

NeeCee gawked. "That's an outhouse?"

I looked at the clearing. "I'll keep a look out while you pee if you will while I do," I said.

She shook her head. "I'm not going in that thing!"

I laughed. "And you think I will? No ma'am! The forest floor is just as good. Seriously, just watch out, will you?"

She nodded, and I found a place to relieve myself before giving her a chance to do the same. It was freezing inside the forest, and there was snow everywhere. The trees over the cottage were bare and covered in ice. A trail led from the rotted cabin steps into the forest beyond, and the trees opened up to reveal a clearing with a sparkling lake in the distance. I was in my vision again, only this time, I wasn't seeing the past.

I lifted the quilt I'd stolen from the cabin, gripping it harder than necessary. With my backpack, the added cover was bulky and heavy, but I didn't have a jacket and I refused to freeze.

I moved forward with NeeCee on my heels.

"Are we in Scotland you think?" she asked.

I nodded. I had no doubt that's where we were. I knew this place.

Voices met us as we moved down the trail to the clearing beyond. I paused behind a tree, my eyes on the Demon, the Angel, and the witch beyond. Another woman stood with them. She was old, her back bent. Thin, white hair trailed down her shoulders, and she had on several layers of plain brown clothing and a thick brown cloak.

A fire crackled inside a circle of grey, smooth stones.

Luther looked up from where he was standing, his eyes going to the trees, and I knew he felt me there, had probably felt me the moment I'd opened my eyes. It both bothered me and comforted me. If this wasn't proof of my possession, nothing was. I had no doubt Luther had been inside the vision with me when we were back in Belle's living room. How else would he know where this place was?

Luther gestured at me, and I stepped out of the protection of the trees. NeeCee followed.

The elderly woman looked up, and I stared. She looked so much like my mother, only much, much older, that it was frightening. Her old eyes found my face, and the wrinkles around her mouth moved as she smiled. It was a forced smile. There was no warmth there.

"The cursed ones," the woman croaked.

My boots sloshed through snow as we approached the warmth of the fire.

"It's so very nice to meet you too," I replied, my gaze moving over the group curiously.

It wasn't long past dawn, and the sky was grey. If there was a sun, it was hidden under several layers of clouds. It made the dark lake beyond look much colder and dangerous than it probably was.

"This is Hannah," Belle introduced. "She's an Ayers witch."

I wanted to tell her "duh," but just managed to control myself. I studied the old woman cautiously, and her deep blue eyes met mine, her gaze steady and cool.

"If you are an Ayers witch, then why are you not with one of the Covens?" I asked.

The woman stared into the fire. "There are many branches of us, child. A good deal of us choose not to practice as a group. We do not seek out the family Covens. We are solitary practitioners. We practice alone."

"You're an eclectic witch," I said.

There was disdain in my voice. No judgment, just disdain. I had nothing against solitary witches but Hannah was an Ayers. She looked too much like the rest of the women in my family not to be. Why, if she were part of such a strong lineage, would she choose to practice alone?

Hannah limped to me, her old frame bringing her an inch under my chin. Her sharp eyes looked up into mine, and I froze. There was
a lot of magic in her gaze. Strong magic.
"If what you have learned thus far about your own family hasn't led you to solitary
practice then you haven't learned enough," she stated.

Belle drew herself up behind the woman, her face hard. "I take offense to that," Belle argued.

Hannah didn't spare her a glance. Her eyes stayed on mine. "That's because you are no Ayers, young one. You are simply an initiate."

"I am a witch," Belle intoned.

Hannah took a step back, her odd stare finally breaking from mine. I was left feeling strangely bereft.

She faced Belle.

"You are an initiate," the old woman repeated. "Have you fought yet? Have you been faced with Hunters? Have you had to kill or protect your own?"

Belle didn't answer. Her gaze slid away from the old woman's, and Hannah laughed. It was an eerie sound, hollow and weary. I hoped fervently she wouldn't look back at me again because I knew, if she did, I wouldn't be able to look her in the eye.

Unlike Belle, I had seen death. I had joined with my mother's Coven to help protect my best friend, Dayton, in a battle with Demons, and I had fought alongside Dayton, Luther, and Lucas in battles I wished now to forget. It's how I'd learn to craft the amulets.

"And you," Hannah said. She was facing me now, but I kept my gaze averted, my eyes on the fire inside the stone circle by the lake. "You have fought, but not for your own blood. For a friend."

I looked up. From the corner of my eye I could see Luther, Lucas, and NeeCee watching us silently. Luther's face was impassive, Lucas' was knowing, and NeeCee's was uncertain. Behind Hannah, Belle fumed.

"Are you a visionary then?" I asked.

"Aye," the woman answered. "Same as you."

She moved closer. I wanted to back away, but I held my ground. Her gaze tried to catch mine, and I wouldn't let it. It was bad enough I had a Demon in my head, I wouldn't let her into it as well.

"The friend is like a sister to me. She is family," I said quietly. Dayton and I were much more than friends to each other. Much more.

"And so it is so. You are not like the rest of the cursed in our line, Ellie Elizabeth Jacobs," Hannah revealed.

This time, my gaze did meet hers, my eyes wide, shocked.

"The rest?" I asked.

She nodded. "It is why you have come, isn't it? To discover why you carry your link with Demons, why your cousin here attracts the Hunters?"

Belle took a step closer to Hannah, but the old woman held up a hand, stopping her, her eyes only for me.

"I know little. Our family's secrets have long since passed into the hands of the cursed among us. But I do know one thing." The old woman's brown cloak moved around her as her thick, brown leather boots met mine in the snow. "While you are *not* the first Demon-cursed Ayers, you *are* very different from those who came before you."

My gaze was trapped by Hannah's.

"How so?" I whispered, my voice hoarse.

One of Hannah's wrinkled hands came up to my face, her rough skin touching my cheek. Compared to my own skin, her palm was warm.

"You," she said, "are not evil."

Chapter 11

I've taken to getting up just past dawn and walking down to the river every morning. I keep waiting for my aunt to say something, to tell me the walk is either too long or too dangerous alone, but she doesn't. I always stop at the railing between the aquarium and the River Walk mall. I like the way the wind feels near the river, the way the sun rises over the water as boats move out into the current. As a witch, nature calls to me, but the river speaks. Its dark and dangerous waters are alluring. I've had a vision about this river. I'm on it, and it is sunset. Behind me, there is a man, his arms wrapped around my waist. I'm beginning to think I am crazy. My visions make no sense.

~Monroe's Totally Wicked Book of Shadows~

I was having a hard time processing the old woman's words. Evil?

Luther stepped up beside me. "It's as I suspect then?" he asked.

I looked up at him. As he suspected? What did he suspect?

Hannah looked at him. "It is not something I can confirm. All I know is that the women in our family before Ellie who carried the Demon curse were not good women. They were dangerous to themselves and to our family."

"Monroe," I corrected. Why my nickname seemed so important to me now, I had no idea, but it did.

Hannah grinned. This time the smile was genuine. "You even shirk the name of your predecessors."

"The name?" I asked. "Those before me shared my name?"

Hannah nodded. "Some of them did."

I was getting impatient, my heart thudding in my chest, and I felt Luther's hand rest firmly on my shoulder.

"What happened to them?" Luther asked. "Where are these cursed women now?"

Hannah laughed. "You don't know, Demon?"

Luther's eyes narrowed. "Speak, woman. Unlike the Ayer witch standing next to me, I am not kind or patient."

Hannah's glacial blue eyes met his. "They are in Hell, Demon, enjoying the wonderful lakes of fire I'm sure you were born in."

Luther's hand tightened on my shoulder.

"No," I gasped.

Hannah's eyes were filled with sympathy when they met mine again. "It is the fate of your kind. Unless your Demon here can save you, you will join them eventually. You will have no choice."

I could feel the sob working its way up into my chest, but I fought it.

"And me?" NeeCee asked frantically, her panicked tone breaking into the tension. "What about me?"

Hannah's saddened gaze moved to my cousin. "It is even more pitiful that the curse of the Hunted should fall on your shoulders, dear. You, who are so afraid. You are fated, as the rest in your line, to die. Fortunately for you, the Hunter-cursed Ayers descendant before you is still alive."

NeeCee was shaking uncontrollably now, and Lucas let one of his arms fall across her shoulders, his eyes soft. He may be fallen, but he was still an Angel. It was in his nature to offer comfort.

"What do you mean still alive?" Belle asked.

The old witch's gaze skirted the group. "The last witch cursed with calling powers took her fate into her own hands and did something none of us would dare do." Hannah moved to the fire, her hand lifted. "She turned on her own kind and joined the Hunters to save herself."

This time even Belle gasped.

"And that makes me fortunate?" NeeCee cried.

Hannah looked at her. "It does, sweet one. Because she, unlike most Hunters, may show you pity."

I could do nothing more than stare.

"How did this happen to us?" I asked Hannah. "What did the Ayers do that was so bad?"

The old witch waved her hands over the fire, some kind of powder falling from her palms. It made the blaze *poof* upward, smoke billowing around us.

"Asked the cursed, Ellie Jacobs. Ask them what we did wrong."

And with that, the old woman was gone, the smoke swallowing her up, leaving nothing more than empty air in her place.

Belle waved her hands over the spot Hannah had stood. "What the hell?"

Luther's hand dropped from my shoulder as NeeCee turned her head into Lucas' chest, her shaking shoulders obvious. I didn't blame her for her tears. Normal people cried.

I walked over to the fire. It was burning low now, the powder used by Hannah spread out on the ground below. I leaned down and touched it carefully. My fingertips tingled.

"Witch powder," I said, my voice low. "Many witches have their own recipes. It's mainly used for show. The real magic was in her disappearance. How she did that is beyond me."

Luther leaned down next to me. "Not magic. All psychological. She merely bent your perception. She is able to manipulate what humans see. She could be standing next to you, and you wouldn't know. It's one of her gifts."

I looked over at him. "But you can still see her? Is she still here now?"

"She isn't far," Luther answered, his eyes going to the forest. "But we are done with her. No need to detain her."

My mouth fell open. "Done with her! But there are so many questions that haven't been answered!

Luther's eyes went to Lucas. The fallen Angel shook his head. "You forget," Luther said, "that Lucas has the ability to read thoughts if he so wishes. There was nothing in the witch's head that she didn't already reveal to us. She's right. We need to find the cursed."

I stiffened. The cursed?

I let go of the blanket at my neck, my hand going to Luther's bare arm. Even in the cold, his skin was warm. I gripped him.

"We're not going to Hell," I gasped.

I had learned to overcome a lot of fears in my life. Hell was not one of them.

One of Luther's hands came up to cover mine. "No, not Hell. Not yet." His hand fell away, and he stood, his eyes once again on the forest. "We find the Ayers witch turned Hunter."

Chapter 12

My aunt has been trying an assortment of potions on me, but they are doing nothing more than making me sick. It's the best unintentional diet I've ever been on. I'm not sure what my aunt is hoping to achieve with them. Drinking nasty concoctions can't possibly unlink me to Demons. But I have had one nasty side effect. At night, my dreams are impossibly vivid and completely out of my control. They aren't visions. I know when I'm having a vision. These are dreams. Often, the dreams are about the Demon Luther.

~Monroe's Totally Wicked Book of Shadows~

Luther and Lucas took us back to the cabin in the woods. The kindling inside the stove had burned out while we'd been gone, but a wave of Luther's hand sent flames shooting up from the ash while Lucas threw in more logs from a pile just behind the cabin. Belle searched a set of rough cabinets with curtains hanging over the shelves, and she found several cans of beef stew and a loaf of bread.

"So the old woman lives here?" I asked, my eyes on the supplies in Belle's arms.

"No," Lucas answered, "Although I doubt she lives far. She practices here."

I sat heavily on the iron bed I'd slept in while NeeCee settled in next to me, her head going to my shoulder. I let my own head fall onto hers. I'd grown up with NeeCee chasing after me as children. Even though she lived in New Orleans, and my family lived in Mississippi, we'd traveled there often, not only for rituals but for holidays. Having three older brothers, NeeCee was often like a little sister to me. I felt responsible for her in so many ways.

"I don't want to die," NeeCee whispered.

I glanced down at her. "You won't," I promised fiercely. "You won't."

"I think the old woman is crazy," Belle said, her voice breaking into the quiet tension. "The Ayers are the first witches I've ever heard of being cursed. And it makes no sense. Even when Clara told me about Bernice, and then Monroe showed up with her problem, it made no sense. Evil witches make sense, but cursed?

Luther looked up at her. "You're a practitioner," he said simply.

Belle began digging in the cabinet for a pot, her eyes meeting Luther's before moving away again. "You say that like it's an accusation. Yes, I'm a practitioner. I practice Wicca. So what?"

I prodded NeeCee gently so that she'd allow me to stand. Belle located her pot. The stew cans she held had those easy tabs on the top that eliminated the need for a can opener, and Belle pulled them up, dumping the contents into the cookware before moving toward the wood stove. My eyes followed her.

"There's a big difference between a practitioner and those of us born with witch blood," I said softly.

Belle practically slammed the pot onto the stove's surface before turning to face me, her eyes hard.

"And what is that exactly, Ellie Jacobs? I'm getting awful damned tired of being told I won't understand because I'm either not an Ayers or not a blood witch."

I closed my eyes. "I love my family, but right now, if I could give you my blood, I would," I said.

With that, I walked from the room, leaving even the blanket behind as I hopped down out of the cabin and into the woods. The trees embraced me, but they did nothing to protect me against the biting wind. I would regret my hasty retreat soon, but for now, I found it refreshing. The cold made me human, made me something other than an Ayers, made me something other than a curse. I headed for the lake, the late morning sun having burned some of the grey away, leaving the sky more azure than overcast.

I sensed him before I reached the clearing. Even without my powers, something about him drew me.

"I can't even have this moment?" I asked.

The lake was in front of me again, and Luther was leaning against a tree just at the edge of the tree line. Damn he was fast!

"No," Luther said. "Not now."

I passed him, and he followed me. The air around me was suddenly warmer, the snow beneath the Demon's feet melting away with each step.

"And Lucas let you come?" I asked lightly.

Luther laughed. "The Angel couldn't stop me if he wanted to. Lucas and I have our differences, but we both know this is my domain."

I turned to look at him. "That *I'm* your domain, you mean."

His dark eyes stared at me from under brooding lids. It didn't seem fair that Luther could possess me, that he could see into my head, into my past, but I couldn't do the same. A one-sided battleground is no place for a fight.

"Hell," Luther said. "Hell is my domain. And according to the old witch, those Demon-cursed among you end up there."

He stopped next to the stone ring that held the fire from earlier. Flames shot up, the blaze brighter than fire should ever be.

I stared at Luther's profile. "You don't like witches do you?" I asked.

Luther stiffened, and I moved to stand next to him, the wind making my hair wild around my head. I should be cold, but I wasn't. Luther was doing something to keep me warm.

"What has made you hate us so much?" I asked him.

He looked down at me. "I don't hate witches."

I thought about his reaction at Belle's apartment the day before. *"What would either of you know about witchcraft?" Belle asked. Luther laughed, the sound harsh, cold. His eyes were red when they met Belle's. "Witch, we've been around long before your people's first sacred circle."*

"You certainly aren't fond of us," I argued.

Luther's green eyes were suddenly tinged red. It was funny really. Red on green. It made me think of Christmas, of candy canes and jolly old elves. Luther was the antithesis of all that.

"I have no problems with witches," he repeated. "I have a problem with people who think they are witches. Who find the idea of power tantalizing, and then abuse it."

I stared up at him, my eyes searching. "Those aren't witches," I said.

The smirk he gave me was cold. "No, they aren't."

Luther walked to the edge of the lake, water licking the tips of the black combat boots he wore.

"What did they do to you?" I asked. "These people who called themselves witches?"

Luther laughed. "You don't let things go do you?"

I picked up a rock from the bank and threw it into the lake. Where the stone fell, water rippled out, making first small rings and then larger ones. Being an Ayers witch was like those circles. Sometime during the past, an Ayers witch messed up, and it has had catastrophic consequences since, wrapping us in rings we can't escape.

"You're inside my head, Demon," I pointed out. "I have no doubt you know exactly how hot I like my bath water, how many teaspoons of sugar I like in my coffee, which side I like to sleep on, what I'm afraid of ... give me something about *you* to trust. Something. Give me a reason not to find a way to break away from you and Lucas, to not take Bernice and figure this problem we have out on our own. What did those witches do to you?"

I knew, in all actuality, it would probably be impossible for Bernice and I to run, but the bravado felt good.

Luther leaned over and touched the lake's surface, cupping the liquid before lifting his hand. Steam rose from his skin as water fell through his fingers.

He looked at me over his shoulder. "I was summoned once by witches."

I froze, fighting to keep my eyes from widening. Summoned. He had been summoned?
Wow. I knew those spells, but I also knew they were forbidden. A witch could summon the Shadows, as we called them, but controlling them was a different story. It's why we had the Rede. Never do anything that could harm ourselves or others. The Shadows were unpredictable, dangerous. They were Demons.

"Speechless now?" Luther asked, his lips quirked.

I swallowed. "What did they make you do?" I whispered.

Again, Luther laughed. "You really want to know?" he asked.

I looked away. If I was being honest, I didn't want to know. I knew why Demons were summoned. It was usually for revenge or something equally deadly. The witches who'd called him weren't witches. They had turned their backs on the Rede.

"And the witches who called you? Where are they now?"

Luther stood, moving next to me, his back to the lake. His arm brushed my shoulder, and I looked up at him. His black hair had fallen onto his forehead, and his eyes were red.

"They're dead," he said. And with that, he smiled. "Did you want to know how dangerous I was, Monroe? Or did you need a real reason to trust me? Because if that's the case, then know
this, I have given you more power over me than I've allowed anyone in a long, long time."

I blinked. "How so?" I breathed.

He leaned closer. "Because you know the name I use in Hell. The same one that can be used to summon me."

I stared at him. I couldn't have broken eye contact even if I wanted to. Thorne. The witches had summoned Thorne.

"Why?" I asked.

The question was vague, but Luther knew what I was getting at.

"Because I owed you. Because once, I stood in front of Lucifer, and your amulet protected me from him. We're more alike than either of us would care to admit, Witch. I don't like being out of control either." He leaned closer still. "And yet sometimes losing control isn't all bad."

Somehow Luther's hand had made its way to my chin, and he gripped it firmly. His lips lowered. I wanted to look away and couldn't.

"Don't make me do this," I begged.

Luther grinned even as my lips parted. "Witch, I'm not in your head right now. What you want now, in this moment, is all you. There's a lot of things I'll take by force. Not that."

His lips crashed down onto mine, and I didn't fight him. I didn't fight him because he was right. I wanted this.

His free hand went to my waist, playing with the skin just under the hem of my t-shirt, and I plunged my fingers into his hair. I had planned on pulling him away, but I gripped his head instead, allowing him to deepen the kiss even as my other hand found its way to his back, fisting the fabric of his t-shirt, the move as desperate as the kiss. The muscles under his shirt were tight, restrained, and I knew then he was holding back.

The kiss, the moment, was so wrong, and yet that's precisely what made it so right. For *this* moment, I wasn't broken, I wasn't cursed, I wasn't a witch. I was Monroe, the vintage loving control freak kissing a man I was reasonably attracted to. Only he wasn't a man, and I wasn't just a girl.

Luther pulled me into him, and my hands moved to his face, my palms keeping his mouth trapped against mine. He growled, the sound primal as his hands gripped my hips painfully, one palm making its way slowly, *oh so slowly*, up to my ribs. I leaned into the touch.

A sound made me freeze.

Luther pulled away, his eyes trapping mine to his face even as I caught a glimpse of Belle at the edge of the clearing. My cheeks flamed.

"Sometimes," Luther whispered as Belle's figure disappeared. "being bad is better."

And with that, he released me. I almost stumbled to the ground, but caught myself, my eyes on anything but Luther.

"Tell me something really stupid or mundane about you," I said breathlessly. It seemed such a silly thing to say, and yet I needed something from him, something that made him more human than what he claimed to be.

I knelt on the lake's bank, one hand on the ground, an arm across my middle. My heart raced.

Luther knelt next to me. "I collect baseball caps."

I choked on the laugh that escaped. My eyes came back up to his. "Baseball caps?"

He shrugged. "I don't wear them. I just collect them. I like them."

I laughed, and this time I couldn't stop. It bubbled up and just kept coming.

Luther stood, his hand out. "It was just a kiss, Monroe. I didn't steal your soul."

I looked at his offered palm, my laughter turning to coughs.

I pushed myself up without taking his hand. "To be on the safe side, let's not do that again," I said.

Luther's lips twitched as I moved past him, my steps carrying me back toward the cabin.

"Oh, Witch," Luther chuckled. "I don't ever make promises like that."

Chapter 13

In my dreams, Luther Craig isn't just the wise crack Demon I met in Italy when Marcas and Dayton were trying to get unbound. He is in a dark, fiery place searching for something. There are shadows surrounding him, and they are screaming. They are sad and in pain. Something about it doesn't sit well with the Demon. His face lifts, and I wake up.

~Monroe's Totally Wicked Book of Shadows~

Belle wouldn't meet my gaze when we returned to the cabin, and I didn't blame her. NeeCee was just as I'd left her, the only difference a small cracked bowl full of canned stew in her hands.

Lucas' gaze met Luther's when we entered the room, a frown on his lips. "Any trouble?" he asked.

Luther grinned. "None."

Lucas' frown deepened. Belle took a seat beside NeeCee, her eyes on me, as if she were warning me away from my own cousin. She'd seen me kiss a Demon. Maybe she thought I was corrupted now.

"You said before you thought we should find the Hunters," Belle said, her eyes on me, but her words for Luther. "How do we do that?"

Luther glanced between Belle and I as Lucas stepped forward.

"Fallen Angels and Demons are limited somewhat here on Earth. We can do a lot, but only you can locate the Hunters," Lucas said.

Belle looked at the Angel. "How?"

"Divination," NeeCee answered quietly. She looked calm when she glanced up, her eyes red but tear free, empty. Crying could do that. It could empty out a person until there was nothing left but cold determination.

Belle studied us all. "So we scry?" she asked. NeeCee nodded.

Belle stood, moving to the center of the cabin, her eyes on the floor. "We'll need a bowl of water," she stated.

Lucas took a dark, chipped bowl from the cabinet, his brows raised. "Sometimes it sucks being fallen." He disappeared then only to return moments later with the bowl full of lake water. Belle's eyes went wide. Lucas grinned. "I'm an Angel. My talents before I fell far exceeded Demon boy's here. If it weren't for the fall, I'd be able to find your Hunters without the help of dinnerware."

"Your fault, Angel," Luther said.

He was leaning against the cabin wall behind me, his arms crossed.

"Yeah, well ..." Lucas shrugged. "Things happen."

Belle raised her brows but didn't say anything as she took the bowl. NeeCee had already moved from the bed to the floor, and I moved next to her, sitting Indian-style as Belle placed the bowl before us. She sat opposite us, thanking the Goddess, her voice high and clear.

I leaned over the bowl, my reflection in the water. NeeCee and Belle leaned with me, their wide-eyed gazes next to mine.

I let my mind wander, my body slipping into the realm of meditation I had been taught to seek the day I told my mother I wanted to follow in her Wiccan footsteps. It was a nice place, *my* place, the peaceful part of my brain where I'd learned to let everything go. It was harder to find it with Luther in the room. I found myself wondering more than once if he was in that place with me now. I hoped not. It was mine.

The water in the bowl stirred, and our faces were replaced with darkness, a blackness far darker than night. NeeCee stiffened next to me, and I reached down to grip her hand. She had my curse now, and I hers. It couldn't hurt to touch her.

A face appeared in the bowl. NeeCee jumped, and I clutched her tighter. The face before us was female. She was middle-aged with blonde hair tied tightly in a bun on top of her head. The woman's brows were creased, her eyes widening when her gaze mets ours in the water. It was obvious she could see us and that meant only one thing.

Belle sat up. "What the he—"

The woman in the water began to speak, her mouth moving silently. My gaze followed her lips, her words obvious to me, and I leaned over to grip the bowl, my hand slipping from NeeCee's.

"Oh, no you don't!" I cried, my unblinking eyes locked on the reflection.

NeeCee leaned over next to me. "Monroe?" she asked.

I didn't break eye contact with the unknown woman. She had a small braid in her hair, tied up into the bun. In my mind's eye, I could see the red-haired Hunter again from the vision in Belle's living room. He'd had a braid too.

"She is an Ayers, no doubt," I said. "Same hair color, same eyes." I paused. "And she is our Hunter."

NeeCee's hand went to my shirt. "How do you know?" she breathed.

I could feel Luther and Lucas at my back, but they kept away from the water. It wouldn't do for the woman in the bowl to see them.

I narrowed my eyes, my voice lowering, my gaze on the woman's braid. "Hunter," I said. The woman in the water sneered, and I grinned. "I'm right, aren't I?" I asked the reflection.

"Monroe," Belle said firmly.

I ignored her. I wasn't letting the woman in the bowl go. I was on my knees now, my face only an inch above the bowl.

I spoke slowly. "Who are you?" I asked.

The woman began to pull away, and for the first time since the store disaster, I dared to use NeeCee's magic. I chanted under my breath, my words calm, steady.

Belle gasped. "Monroe, no!"

But I didn't stop. I had more confidence than NeeCee. I knew now what her magic was capable of, and I was determined to reign it in. The woman in the water froze, immobile, and I grinned wickedly.

"Who are you?" I insisted.

The woman's hands went up to her neck as if she was choking, her face going red. She was fighting my magic, but I wasn't letting her go. I believed completely in the Rede. I would not harm her, but this woman had harmed other witches, her own family, and I wouldn't let her go until I knew where to find her. I may not be a Demon with the power to possess someone, but I was a witch, and I knew a damned good coercion spell.

The woman's lips moved, and I stared at them. Mary? Mandy?

"Maggie," Luther said from behind me.

I grinned again. "Maggie," I repeated. "Where are you, Maggie?"

The woman in the water struggled, her eyes narrowing as she focused on me. I knew what she planned to do before she did it, but I still didn't drop the bowl.

The electric shock that went through me was strong, painful, and I grit my teeth as my hold on Maggie broke. Her face disappeared, but I kept my eyes on the water, whispering frantically.

"Her location," I begged the dark surface.

And then there it was. A town. I didn't recognize it at all, but I felt the subtle shift in my brain, my place of peace, when Luther suddenly intruded. His presence was heavy, and I wondered now why I'd not felt him before.

"*Because he hadn't been in my peaceful place*," I answered myself. But he was there now, and he was seeing the same town I was.

The bowl fell out of my hands, shattering on the wooden floor in front of me. I was weak, and my hands went down into the glass. I winced when one of the shards pierced my skin.

"Ah," I heard Luther growl as he moved away from me, his eyes red.

NeeCee lifted my hand and pushed a corner of her blanket onto my cut. "You okay?" she asked.

I nodded, my hair over my face. Luther was near the door now, his hand tight on the frame. I could see his knuckles turning white from where I knelt. Blood. He liked the taste of blood.

"Did you find out where the woman was?" Belle asked.

I shook my head. "I saw a place. A town."

"Salem," Luther breathed.

I looked up, my eyes meeting his. His jaw was tight, but he looked better, more in control.

Lucas backed away from me, putting his body between me and Luther. He didn't seem concerned about Luther's reaction to my blood. There was no doubt he'd seen it many times before with the Demon.

"You've got to be kidding," Lucas said.

Luther snorted. "Seems the Hunters have a nice sense of humor," he said wryly.

Belle stood. "Salem? As in Salem, Massachusetts?"

NeeCee was laughing now, a frantic laugh that spoke of stress and anxiety. She still held the blanket against my palm, and she was pressing it too hard against my skin. I gently pried her fingers off of mine.

"Salem," NeeCee said. "What a perfect place for them to put us on trial."

She laughed even as I lifted her chin with my fingers. "Salem is a haven for witches now, NeeCee."

Luther was suddenly kneeling next to me, his face turned away from my injured hand. "And we are the hunters this time, remember?" he said.

I looked at him, at the way his red eyes looked at NeeCee, and I suddenly knew he was in her head. She went from anxious to calm in the blink of an eye. Much calmer than she'd been before, her laughter gone.

Luther's eyes moved to mine.

"No," I mouthed.

He stared at me. "You two swapped magic, Monroe. If I don't keep a presence inside of you both, Lucifer will take one of you."

He stood then, moving back so that he was next to Lucas. The Angel watched quietly, and my eyes went wide.

"You *do* know!" I accused. I had thought Lucas was unaware of Luther's possession of me, but I'd been wrong.

Belle stood. "Know what?" she asked.

Lucas looked at me. "The Demon is right, Monroe. If he doesn't keep a steady presence, then you and Bernice will be in a much worse position than you are now."

Belle was getting aggravated. "*What* is going on?" she asked, her voice loud.

I ignored her, my heart plummeting. I'd had no problem with Luther possessing me. I hadn't liked it. I hadn't wanted him inside of me, but I'd been okay with it. I had fought him, yes. But in the end, I'd do anything to keep Lucifer away. But not Bernice.

"She doesn't understand," I whispered, my eyes moving to my cousin.

NeeCee had moved to one of the beds, her eyes glassy. She climbed onto it and rolled into a fetal position.

"She'll never know I was there," Luther said.

Belle had had enough. "What the hell is going on?" she demanded.

I moved to the bed where NeeCee lay, sitting on the edge of it before placing my hand on her back. Her breathing was even, deep. She was sleeping. Vaguely, I heard Lucas talking to Belle, and her angry reply.

"He can't do that!" Belle said.

"I can," Luther responded firmly. "And I will until the power swap spell fades and we find the Hunters."

No one said anything for a long while. I kept my hand on NeeCee's back and listened to the occasional *snap* as logs fell inside the wooden stove, and the *pop* and *crackle* as the blaze changed.

"There's no other way?" I asked.

It was Luther who answered me. "In the long run, I will have done nothing but help her."

Funny. Bernice and I, Demon possessed cursed witches. How much crazier could things get? I was suddenly the girl in that movie *The Exorcist*, and I winced.

"If we start vomiting pea soup, I'll find a way to have your head," I said finally.

Belle snickered. She actually snickered, and it made me grin despite myself. A bowl was shoved abruptly under my face, and I looked up to find Belle standing next to me.

"It's cold," she warned.

I shook my head. "I'm not hungry."

Belle forced it into my hands. She gestured at the Demon and Angel in the room. "They may not have to eat, sleep, or piss, but we do. Eat. You'll thank me later."

I took the bowl and watched as Belle crossed the room toward Lucas and Luther.

"Here's the deal," Belle said. "I wasn't born with witch blood. You know it, I know it. But I have sworn my fealty to the Rede, and Clara took me into her Coven when no one else would. I don't have a stellar history, but I'm a damn good initiate, and Clara trusts me. Don't cross me."

With that, she walked to the empty bed opposite the one I sat on.

Her eyes met mine. "Rest," she ordered. "Just a few hours, and then we are going on our own witch hunt."

She laid back then, turning away from me. My gaze moved to Lucas and then Luther. The Demon's eyes were on the raven-haired witch's back, a new respect in his gaze, and I found myself torn between my own growing respect for Belle and jealousy.

I pushed it away when I saw Luther grin. I couldn't forget he was in my head. I couldn't forget that the only things I knew about him were his lust for blood, the name he used in Hell, his sour past with witches, and his fondness for baseball caps. I clung to the baseball cap image. It made him somewhat human.

I was feeling tired, and I crawled into the bed next to NeeCee. The weariness wasn't natural. My eyes found Luther's again where he stood next to Lucas by the door.

"Don't," I warned.

Luther grinned again. "Sweet, tempting dreams," he said.

My world went black.

Chapter 14

I've been reading the parts of the Ayers grimoire that I can translate. A good deal of it is in Latin, which I'm actually pretty good at reading. The Ayers are powerful witches. In our line, the females hold the most power. This isn't always the case. There are plenty of powerful natural born male witches, but it's the female line in the Ayers family that seems more predisposed to magic. According to the text, most of us survived the witch craze in Medieval Europe, and we traveled to the new world looking for religious freedom. We migrated toward the South, to the land of magnolias and swamps. There is something mysterious about the South. It has hidden us well, cloaked us. I haven't found anything that would connect me to Demons, but there's one part of the book I still can't read. I've tried, but the tingling in my body gets so bad, I have to stop. Only Demons make me hurt like that. Why would the grimoire?

~Monroe's Totally Wicked Book of Shadows~

In the blackness, I dreamed.

Light surrounded me, gentle sunlight burning through an early morning haze. A rolling green field with low stone walls spread out in front of me with a small stone cottage sitting crookedly on the meadow's edge. White, puffy clouds floated above the house, and smoke lifted from a narrow chimney.

I walked toward the home, breathing in the scent of early morning. It was cold, but not as cold as the lake and forest. It was the kind of cold that would heat with the rising sun. Damp grass clung to my boots.

Someone yelled, and I froze.

"Mac! Mac!" a girl screamed.

From the edge of the field, a blonde-haired girl ran down a hill, her hair flying behind her. I knew this girl, and my eyes narrowed. Eta. This girl was Eta. She was an older Eta than the one I'd seen at the lake in my vision, the one who'd watched her father killed by Hunters.

The door to the cottage slammed open, and a broad-shouldered young man stepped out into the sun. His brown breeches and knee-length black boots clung to him. A loose white tunic hung open, his bronze chest bare to the elements. He didn't seem to notice or care, his hand coming up to shield his eyes.

"Eta!" he called out.

The girl flew into Mac's arms, and his shirt tightened over his back as his arms enfolded her, one large hand coming up to the back of her head.

"Shhh ..." he soothed. "What's happened, Lass?"

Eta pulled back, her startling red-rimmed blue eyes going up to Mac's face. Eta was beautiful, her skin ethereal, her features soft and doll-like. I found myself wondering briefly if I looked like that. I certainly didn't see myself that way.

I edged closer to them, my experience with the Hunter in the vision I'd had at Belle's making me cautious. I didn't know if I was dreaming the scene, envisioning it, or participating in it.

Eta's hand came up to Mac's longish, chestnut hair. There were red highlights in his thick mane, and the sun made them glint as Eta ran her fingers through it. The move was familiar, intimate, and it made my chest tighten. What would it feel like to trust someone that deeply?

"It's the Coven, Mac," Eta said after a moment. "They want me to take over for my father."

Mac smiled, his handsome, rugged face transforming. "That's good, is it not?"

Eta didn't share his enthusiasm. "Mac, if I choose to lead them, I'll have to leave. The Hunters have been breathing down our necks now for a while. First, they killed my father and now they have infiltrated the nobility. The witch craze begins. Our Coven ... we will need to leave to escape it."

Mac had grown still, his shoulders tensing. His hand went to Eta's stomach. For the first time, I noticed it was rounded, soft. Eta was pregnant.

"You canna go," Mac said fiercely. "Not now."

Eta's hand moved to Mac's face, to the new growth of whiskers along his chin. I could almost feel its roughness against my own palm, and I clenched my fist, my heart pounding. My hand went to my stomach, my eyes welling up with tears. Somehow, some way, I was inside Eta's head. Her love for Mac was my love, and my heart was breaking.

"The Coven ... most of them are my family. Cousins, aunts, uncles, children ... I cannot let them die."

Mac's hand came up to cover Eta's on his face. "Someone else can lead. I can protect you here. I protected you before."

Eta's hand tightened on Mac's jaw, her eyes searching his. Desperation ran rampant through her blood, *my* blood. "Come with me, Mac," she begged. "For me. For the baby."

Mac's eyes darkened. "This is my land, Eta. My birthright. My family fought for generations for this land, bled for it, and you are asking me to leave it?"

"Aye," Eta whispered. "I am. The witch craze, it won't just kill witches. You must know that. They will accuse anyone associated with us. They will torture you."

Mac stepped away from Eta, and her hands fell to her sides.

"I canna go, Eta. I canna. These men and women are my neighbors. We have shed blood together. We have sweated together. They willna accuse me or you," Mac stated firmly.

Eta stepped toward him. "It willna matter. Magic scares people. They think witches are evil, that we ally ourselves with the devil. Your bond with them willna matter. Please understand—"

"Understand what, Eta? That you want me to leave my land, *my* family to follow you? You are asking me to do the same thing you refuse to do for me. I stood up for you once, protected you when your father died, and you now refuse to stay here with me."

Eta hugged herself, her arms going around her middle. I could feel the baby in her belly moving, like butterfly wings, and I hugged my own middle, the wonder of it completely overwhelming me.

"Please, Mac! Don't make me choose between you and our baby," Eta whispered.

Mac's jaw dropped. "Choose! You think I am asking you to choose?"

Eta nodded. "If I stay, I risk being killed. I risk the baby being killed. Do you not see that?"

"They wouldna do that," Mac argued. "You are safe here. *Our* baby is safe here."

Eta's eyes were sad when she looked at Mac. "I have visions, Mac. You know that. It willna be okay."

Mac went down on his knees, his hands clutching Eta's homespun white dress, the brown cloak she wore over it falling down her shoulders as Mac's head went to

Eta's stomach.

"Don't," he said. "Don't."

I'm not sure even he knew what he was begging for. A tear slid down Eta's cheek, and I knew when the sharp pain blossomed behind my chest what decision she'd made. Her hands went to Mac's hair, and she clutched it.

"Let's go inside," she said, her voice calm. The baby within her moved again, sealing her decision, her fate.

Mac stood, his face hopeful as she led him inside. The door shut.

The dream changed.

It was suddenly dark outside, the bright moon above not quite full but close. An owl hooted as the dark cottage door opened. I caught a glimpse of a low burning fire within as Eta stepped outside, silently shutting the door behind her. Her eyes went to the moon, and her hand went to her belly.

"You know not what I sacrifice for you," she whispered to her child as she scurried away from the cottage.

With each step, her heart tore, bleeding into her chest until I thought we would both die from internal bleeding. But she didn't. I didn't, and I followed her, my booted feet running on slippery grass.

I fell to my knees, my eyes going to Eta's back as she met up with a group of cloaked figures on the hill above the cottage. The Coven.

"You willna be followed?" an older woman asked, her white hair thin where it lay against her brown cloak.

Eta looked back down the hill. "I am a good witch, Maren. He will sleep peacefully tonight."

Maren nodded, her eyes sad. "I am sorry, Eta. You made the right choice."

Eta frowned, anger moving through her veins. "I didna choose the Coven, Maren. Remember that. I do this now for my child."

The woman didn't answer, and the group of cloaked figures moved away again, disappearing into a thick forest at the edge of the field. Eta didn't look back.

Once more, the dream changed.

It was still night, but there was no doubt time had passed. There was thick snow on the ground. Trees were bare. The wind was sharp. I
shivered, but I didn't move. I was near the cottage again, but now there was yelling in the distance and torches bobbing in the blackness beyond.

"Witch lover!" someone screamed.

My heart sunk when the mob appeared on the hill.

The cottage door opened, and a much thinner, broken Mac exited. His skin was bare from the waist up, and his young face was covered with a brown beard, his eyes empty. The red in his hair glistened as torchlight covered his figure.

"Take him!" a man yelled.

Hands were suddenly gripping Mac's arms—hard hands, large hands, frightened hands. Mac went down on his knees as a rope was wrapped around his wrists and then his body.

A big burly man tied Mac's hands to the back of a wagon that materialized from the edge of the group. Horses with fur covered feet were harnessed to the front of it, stamping impatiently, their breaths misting on the black air.

"John," Mac said weakly. "Why?"

"Because you dallied with a witch, brother," the big man said. "You are as evil now as they are. Your seed has been passed to the devil."

Mac's head hung, but his biceps tightened where his fists clenched inside the ropes. "I am all the better for it," Mac said. "She was right, and I was a fool."

I fell in love with this man then, this broken man who, even in this moment, didn't turn his back on Eta. It would be his death.

"*Are* you better for it?" John sneered.

Mac looked up, his cold, grey eyes hard. "I am *much* better for it. You can kill me, brother, but you canna destroy my spirit."

John spat in Mac's face. "Now!" John ordered angrily.

The driver of the wagon snapped the horses' reins. I looked away as Mac's body was dragged behind the conveyance. I never heard him scream.

The wagon stopped, and another wagon came up behind it, facing in the opposite direction. My hand came up to cover my mouth as Mac's feet were tied to the new vehicle. They were going to tear Mac's body apart!

"Any last words, brother?" John asked.

Mac couldn't lift his head, but his voice was clear when he said, "If I am a sinner, then so be it. A plague on you all!"

The reins on both carts *snapped.*

I sat up, my scream loud.

A hand went over my mouth. "Shhhh ... wake up, Monroe," Luther's voice said in my ear.

My eyes went wide. The room we were in was dark, but it wasn't the cabin in the Scottish forest anymore. It was a bedroom, a nice one with modern furniture, a roll top desk in the corner, and a large fire in a gas fireplace in front of the bed.

"We traveled while you slept."

Luther answered my unspoken question, his hand still against my lips.

"We are in Salem, in the home of a seer. Belle is downstairs with Lucas. Bernice is asleep in the room next to yours."

Luther's explanation did nothing to calm me. The dream was still too raw, a vivid memory now etched into my brain. I tried backing up and froze when my arm hit my backpack.

My eyes traveled to the bed as Luther's hand slipped away from my face. The blankets over my legs were thick and warm and smelled faintly of Gain laundry detergent, but the pillows were gone, replaced by my backpack, the same backpack that held the grimoire. I didn't look back up at Luther.

"You put the grimoire under my head?"

My words were more an accusation than a question. I was a visionary. I knew now why I'd had the newest vision, knew now it was because Luther had let me sleep on the book.

"Getting inside your family's head is the best way to figure out where they went wrong, and you are the key to that. The Demonic portion of the book is opening to you," Luther said.

I still didn't look at him, a tear working its way from the corner of my eye to my chin. It hung there.

"You suspect the Ayers summoned a Shadow, don't you?" I asked. "You think that's why we are connected to Demons. That we summoned one the same way you were summoned."

The conversation and kiss I'd shared with Luther at the lake was as fresh as the vision I'd just had. Things

Luther had said to Hannah ... it all made sense.

Luther shifted. "It's one of the more obvious reasons for your family's connection to Demons."

My hand lifted, and I placed it against the backpack, on the figures standing arm in arm across the front. The tin man, the cowardly lion, the scarecrow. One looking for a heart, another a brain, and the last for courage. The book lay beneath. My heart bled. *Mac*.

"It doesn't explain Bernice," I said.

Luther didn't answer me. He knew I was right. My hand tightened against the backpack.

"Eta took over the Coven after her father's death. She was pregnant. She was in love. And Mac ... " my voiced cracked. "Mac died for her."

"I know," Luther said, and I looked up at him, at his strong face where the firelight played across his features.

"Why?" I asked. "Why do I need to relive it all?"

Luther's head lowered. "Because your powers are tied to theirs, Monroe. Because the visionaries before you suffered, because they saw things that led to this moment, to whatever it is that cursed your family."

I knew Luther had been in my head. Not only did he *have* to posses me for my *supposed* own good, but I knew he'd want to see what I saw, that he *had* seen what I had seen. It was in his eyes.

"Do you feel nothing?" I asked him. "My heart ... it hurts."

Luther's jaw tightened. "It'll heal," he said.

It seemed so wrong that I was so attracted to this man, this Demon whose hard eyes had probably seen so much more than I had seen in visions, who saw being bad as something good, who seemed untouched by simple moments. But I *was* attracted to him. There was no way I could deny that, not sitting this close to him.

"I'm not sure I want to see more," I whispered.

Luther's hand went to the back of my head. He seemed to have no trouble touching me. I'm not sure he had trouble touching anyone. Luther lived life the way he wanted to live it. No rules. No thought to what was right.

"All of that pain in one witch," he said. I knew he meant me by the way his red-tinged eyes met mine. "It all leads to you. Even Bernice. I don't know how yet, Monroe, but it does."

The interest in his gaze was new. My eyes narrowed. The look didn't mean he was interested in me. Oh, I had no doubt he was attracted to me, but I'd also seen lust in his eyes
with Belle. Hadn't I? No, *this* was something different.

"I'm not a favor you're doing for your brother any more, am I?" I asked.

A smile tugged at Luther lips. "Call it curiosity," Luther said. "Let's just say your family has intrigued me."

And with that, Luther leaned forward, his lips brushing my forehead. It wasn't a sweet kiss. It wasn't even romantic.

"Your blood," he said, "is tempting."

I pulled away. "I won't share it."

Luther laughed. "Doesn't mean I wouldn't love a taste, Witch. You look like an angel, but you smell like trouble. It's damned intoxicating."

I pushed the covers away and stepped over the side of the bed. I was tired of the clothes I was in, and I picked up the backpack. Luther was by the door when I turned, his speed both intimidating and a relief.

"There is a bathroom in the hall. Come downstairs when you are done," he ordered.

I nodded as he moved from the bedroom, the door shutting behind him, leaving me in a room touched by firelight, by images of Mac. My hand went to my flat stomach. Nothing moved within my womb as it had Eta's. I looked up.

"You are the father of one of my ancestors, Mac," I said. "And I am proud to know your blood runs within my veins."

An image of a smiling Mac played behind my eyes as I re-opened the bedroom door and peered out into the hallway before stepping out onto a beautiful wine-colored runner covering deep, mahogany wooden floors. A deep breath, and I closed the bedroom door. Mac's face disappeared.

Chapter 15

Visions are awful things. I say this lightly because, according to my family, it is a gift. Witches with visionary abilities were once considered Oracles in the ancient world. But, if I am being honest with myself, then I must admit that I consider my visions more a curse than I do my Demonic connection. Visions have robbed me of my youth. No one could see the things I do and still feel young. My first vision was of death, the second of my best friend, and since then I have had many dark, frightening visions that make no sense. Like the river I walk to every morning, they are muddy, strong currents that are pulling me under.

~Monroe's Totally Wicked Book of Shadows~

I walked out of the bathroom half an hour later with a damp, hastily done ponytail and pink scrubbed skin while wearing another pair of skinny jeans, and an oversized white, off-the-shoulder sweatshirt with an image of a lounging Marilyn Monroe on the front. It felt nice to be clean, but the shower hadn't helped wash away any of the haunting images I was plagued with now.

Shadows seemed to follow me down the house's twisted, hardwood staircase, and I glanced over my shoulder repeatedly as I searched the lower floor for Lucas, Luther, and Belle.

The house was old and large, the walls and furniture testament to another time period. There were fireplaces in every room, and old glass lighting. The floors were all wood with sporadic throw rugs that matched the individual rooms; browns, wine colors, maroons, creams.

Something pushed me from behind, and I stumbled into a room I hadn't seen my first time through. Two brown stuffed leather chairs sat in front of a picture window on opposite sides of a round mahogany end table holding a large, caramel-shaded lamp. Bookshelves lined the back wall, and the center of the room was dominated by a chandelier highlighting a massive pool table.

Luther leaned against the green felt, a cue stick in one hand while Lucas leaned next to him, his lower lip clenched between his teeth as he gazed at the cue ball critically. Belle stood behind them, her arms crossed and her exasperated eyes on the ceiling. It didn't look like a friendly game of pool.

I ignored them all, my gaze on the hallway beyond. Someone had pushed me. I hadn't seen him, but I'd felt the hands.

"A spirit," a man said.

I stiffened, my eyes moving to the room. Luther and Lucas had straightened, their focus now on the door, on me. Belle looked relieved.

A thin, scarecrow-like man stepped from the room's shadows, the faint sun coming through the picture window making his skin seem pale. He had a thin face with short brown hair, and gold wire-rimmed spectacles perched on the tip of his nose.

"A spirit?" I asked.

The man nodded, his thin lips turned up into a smile. "We have many of them in Salem. You grow used to them," he said as he approached me, his hand outstretched. "I am Henry. You must be Ellie Jacobs."

I took his hand, my gaze on my reflection in his spectacles.

"Monroe," I corrected him. "It's nice to meet you."

His grin widened. "Likewise."

Belle moved around the table, her eyes bright. She had changed while I'd been asleep and was wearing flared jeans, and a fitted red v-neck sweater. Her thick, black hair was pulled back into a ponytail as hasty as mine.

"Henry here can tell the difference between mortals, Angels, and Demons. Something about auras," Belle said, awed.

I grinned. I had met a seer before, a woman named Maria in Italy, but a seer's ability never failed to amaze me.

I nodded at Henry. "Do witches have auras?" I asked. I'd always wondered that but had never thought to ask.

Henry gestured at Belle. "No different than most humans," he answered. "Even those with witch blood." Belle looked disappointed. Henry stepped toward me, his small eyes larger than they should be behind his glasses. "Except for yours. Your aura is different," he said.

Luther laid his cue stick down and moved next to me, his eyes on Henry. "How different?" Luther asked.

Henry sighed. "It's why you came, I understand. And now that I look at her, I see why you'd want to know." His eyes skirted my figure. "Your aura is red with touches of black."

Luther's eyes narrowed. "That's not possible, Henry."

The man laughed. "It shouldn't be, but it is."

I glanced between them. "Is there something wrong with that?"

Lucas had moved next to Luther, and their eyes met, a thought passing between them.

"I wonder why Maria never mentioned it," Lucas murmured.

Henry snorted. "Maria Mancini? She is a legend among seers. She is also considered a little odd. A rebel in many ways, even in her old age."

"And you aren't?" Luther asked. "The fact that you will even allow a Demon in your home makes you as eccentric as Maria. She kept this from us. Why?"

Henry's expression became guarded, unsure. "If Maria Mancini said nothing, then I'm not sure I should either."

Luther's eyes went red, *blood* red. "Maria has two advantages you don't, Seer. She was once my brother's lover, and she has earned her place by guarding treasures of Solomon with her life. *You* have earned nothing. It would be wise for you to talk."

Henry stared. "You threaten me, Demon? Here? In my home."

Luther took a step forward. "Do you think I care where you die, Seer? I think you mistake me for my brother."

"Luther," Lucas warned.

Henry backed away, his skin pale.

"Tell us," Luther insisted.

The room grew cold, frigid even. My breath misted in front of me. I'd never seen a Demon do that before, and I felt the hairs on my arms stand to attention. Fear coursed through me.

"The spirits," Henry whispered, his eyes on the air.

There were hands on my shoulders again, and then they were gone. Spirits? Ghosts? Seriously! I glanced around me, but there was nothing. Only cold air and fear.

Luther smiled. "They are lost souls, Henry. Demons can call on lost souls. Do you want to see what I can make them do?"

Henry wheezed. "You have much of your mother in you, Demon," he gasped.

Luther chuckled. "Yes, I do."

The Demon made no apology, and Henry moved to the nearest leather chair. He sat heavily, and Belle, who'd been on the side of the pool table nearest the chairs, moved as far away from Henry as she could, her arms folded across her middle. The fear in her eyes was stark.

"I'll tell you," Henry conceded. He wheezed again while patting his blue jean pockets. "Just make it stop. Please."

Lucas placed a hand on Luther's shoulder. "Show's over," he said. "Quit scaring the man."

The room returned to its normal temperature, but Luther's eyes stayed red, his body rigid. Whatever spirits had been floating among us seemed to retreat and Henry's breathing returned to normal. Or mostly normal anyway.

"Was that necessary?" Henry asked, his hand going to his chest. "I have asthma, you know."

Luther's eyes glowed, and Henry waved his hands.

"Never mind." Henry wheezed, his gaze moving to me. "The black in Monroe's aura is the mark of a Demon. All Demons have a black aura. But the red ..." Henry's eyes went to Luther. "I have seen the red in mortals, but not the red I see in Monroe. I've only seen the kind of red in Monroe's aura once before."

Luther leaned forward. "I'm not going to like the answer, am I?" he asked.

Henry placed a hand on the chair's armrest. "I suppose that depends. I have a feeling you already know the answer."

Luther swore and looked away as Lucas strode forward. "Enlighten those who don't know," the fallen Angel insisted.

Henry looked at the floor, his hand tightening on the chair until his knuckles were white. "I've only seen that color with the Demon Lilith."

I gasped. I couldn't help myself. "Oh, my God!"

Belle was confused. "Lilith?" she asked.

I swallowed hard. "In myth, Lilith was the first wife of Adam," I explained. "She refused to submit to Adam, and she fled the Garden of Eden, eventually becoming a succubus she-Demon. Later, she lay with the cursed Cain and together they beget many half-breed or hybrid Demons."

"In myth?" Luther said with a laugh. "If you'd been suckled by the bitch, you wouldn't call her a myth."

My gaze went to the Demon. "Luther is one of her children," I told Belle.

There was silence then, a long silence, broken only by the *tick, tick, tick* of a clock somewhere in the house. I hadn't noticed it before, but now it distracted me. *Tick, tick, tick.*

I inhaled. *Tick, tick, tick.* My aura contained the same red color as Lilith's? What did that mean? I exhaled. *Tick, tick, tick.*

"And this red aura means what?" Lucas asked, his question finally breaking the silence.

Henry stood, his stance unsteady. "It means Monroe is connected somehow by blood to the she-Demon."

Luther swore again.

Lucas coughed. "By blood? You jest! As in related?"

I still hadn't spoken. I couldn't. It was taking everything I had just to breathe.

"She's not Lilith's child," Luther stated, his tone adamant.

Henry nodded. "The Demon is right. Monroe doesn't have Lilith's attributes. It's very unlikely she was sired by the Demon."

I finally found my voice. "Then how?" I breathed.

Henry's gaze moved to mine. "Someone in your family is a lilim."

"A *what*?" I asked.

Lucas laughed. "I never would have thought ..." He shook his head.

Belle glared at us all. "What the hell is a lilim?"

Luther turned, his eyes on the room's entrance.

I glanced over my shoulder, my gaze following Luther's. Bernice was on the staircase beyond, her eyes wide behind her glasses.

Her rigid posture and her glassy stare was eerie. *All* of this was eerie.

I glanced around the room at our group—a seer standing shakily by a chair, a fallen Angel laughing at the irony of it all, a Demon with reddened eyes, and three witches without a clue.

"What is a lilim?" Belle asked again.

Luther's eyes moved to mine, his face unreadable. "Lilims are children of Lilith," he said. "But not by blood. *Of* blood. They are women who worship her."

My heart sunk.

"They are women," Luther added, "who trade their souls to her for something in return."

Chapter 16

I've begun to teach myself a little about Hell. It seems foolish not to when I'm constantly haunted by Demons. There is much I already know. I know there are hybrid-Demons, the children of Demons and humans. And I know there are special hybrid children, the sons and daughters of the immortal Cain and the she-Demon Lilith. They are always twins, one of them evil, and the other not so much. And there are many of them. So very many of them. But it is their mother who scares me the most. The she-Demon Lilith is a nasty Demon. I've faced her once when Dayton and Marcas battled Lucifer. My amulet had kept Lucifer from possessing Luther, and Lilith had attacked me. Only Luther jumped in front of me, and my life was spared. But I've thought often on that night. I'd seen a possessive look in Lilith's eyes that still terrifies me.

~Monroe's Totally Wicked Book of Shadows~

Tick, tick, tick.

The women in my family had turned to Lilith? When? Why?

Tick, tick, tick.

I reached behind me, shrugging my backpack off of my shoulder and letting it slide to the floor.

Tick, tick, tick.

I stepped out into the hallway, ignoring NeeCee's strange stare from the stairwell as I searched the hall. There in the corner. A grandfather clock, the pendulum within swinging slowly back and forth.

Tick, tick, tick.

"Monroe?" Belle asked from behind me.

Tick, tick, tick.

My hands found the backpack, the characters of Oz once more staring up at me. I felt like Dorothy, surrounded by people who could benefit from a little bit of courage, heart, and knowledge. Including me.

Tick, tick, tick.

The backpack's zipper was loud in the quiet room, and I went to the floor, my back against the room's entrance as I pulled out the Ayer's grimoire.

Tick, tick, tick.

My eyes went from the grimoire's cracked leather cover to Luther's face. "You told me the book would only reveal itself to me, right?" I asked.

Luther knelt in front of me. "Someone in your family started this, Monroe, but for your aura to be so strongly connected even now to Lilith ..." Luther looked up, his gaze moving over NeeCee, Belle, and then back to me. "Then someone in your family is carrying it on. Someone is still following Lilith, still offering her own family up to the she-Demon in return for something."

My whole body went numb. Somewhere beyond my own shock, I heard Belle gasp. NeeCee stayed silent.

Tick, tick, tick.

I clutched the book to my chest. Images of Mac, a broken Mac, being killed in the name of the Ayers and their Coven replayed in my head. My family. Mac had died for Eta. And before that, Eta's father had died for the Coven at the hands of the Hunters.

Tick, tick, tick.

"She?" I asked, my gaze moving up to Luther's face. "Why would you think it was a woman? There are men in our Coven too. And others. People not related to us."

Luther leaned forward. "Yes, but Lilith deals only with women. She enjoys empowering them. She even enjoys destroying them. And it is still only the Ayers' female bloodline that is cursed. Two women in your line of every generation are dying. One is having blood spilled by the Hunters, and the other is being sacrificed to Lilith herself. Blood and Hell. I should have seen it before. It has my mother's handiwork all over it." Luther looked up at Lucas. "If there was no longer a lilim among the Ayers women, then there would be no witches in this generation cursed for sacrifice. The fact that Monroe and Bernice are both marked means someone is continuing the tradition."

Lucas sighed. "This could be more complicated than we thought."

Belle moved forward. "Maybe I'm naive about all of this, but how is it more complicated?"

I looked down at the book's cover, my fingers playing lightly over the top of it. So many Ayers sacrificed.

"If an Ayers witch summoned Lilith, then we would be subject to her commands," I explained.

I'd spent my whole life listening to my mother talk about Wicca, watching her practice it, studying it with her. The most fascinating and terrifying part of any of her lessons was the Shadows.

My eyes went to Belle's face. "The fact that someone in our family is still summoning her means it's too late for NeeCee and me. If the witch called on Lilith, then her sacrifice must be met."

This time even NeeCee gasped from her place on the stairwell. Nothing Luther could do could calm her now. NeeCee and I were this generation's sacrifice. If my aura was what Henry said it was, then Lilith had already been summoned. We were destined to die, and there was no stopping it.

Tick, tick, tick.

I clenched my jaw, my hand lifting the grimoire's cover. "But there is something we can do."

NeeCee moved down the stairs, her glassy gaze gone, hopeful. "What?" she asked.

I hated to destroy the little hope she had, but I was a practical girl. My hand went to the grimoire's pages, my eyes to Luther's. "We can stop this from happening to the next generation," I said. I knew by the look in Luther's eyes that he knew what I was about to do.

"It's January. It's ..." I looked up at the clock in the hall. *Tick, tick, tick.* "Nine o'clock in the morning." I did this to keep myself grounded, to remind myself that I was still here in this time period.

Luther lowered his head. "Don't talk in the vision," he reminded me.

My eyes stayed locked on his. "Just catch me if I fall."

Chapter 17

I no longer want to sleep. I've taken to spitting all of the concoctions my aunt gives me into the trash when she isn't looking, but days without potions hasn't lessened the dreams. Maybe I was wrong to think the drinks were causing it. I dream often of fire. Worse yet, I dream often of burning.

~Monroe's Totally Wicked Book of Shadows~

A baby cried.

"Shhh ..." a voice soothed.

A rocking chair creaked. Back and forth. Back and forth.

Creak.

"Shhh ..."

Creak.

I was on the porch of a small cabin on the edge of a forest, and it was early, sometime just past dawn. I wasn't a worldly girl, but I was pretty sure this wasn't Scotland anymore. Where, I had no idea, but it wasn't Scotland. Eta wouldn't have stayed in Scotland, but I didn't see her going far either.

The sky was grey, overcast. The baby cried.

Creak.

"Shhh ..."

I looked up, my eyes going to a tired, thin Eta holding a newborn baby with tufts of blonde hair. The infant's face was scrunched and red, its tiny fist wrapped around one of Eta's fingers.

"Shhh ..." Eta said again, her hand running absently down the side of the baby's cheek. It was a beautiful baby, and my heart lurched at the thought of Mac.

The baby's cries turned into wails, and Eta reached up to unfasten the front of her dress. She pulled it down, baring her breasts, and the baby quieted, the suckling sound of the infant's insistent feeding almost comforting in the silence. Only the creaking rocking chair remained.

The cabin door opened, and the old woman from my earlier vision stepped out onto the porch, her gaze hard.

Eta looked up. "Did you see anything?"

Maren nodded. "I've scryed," she said simply.

The creaking rocking chair stopped.

"And?" Eta asked.

Maren sighed. "He's dead, Eta. Between the Hunters and the craze they caused, Mac didna stand a chance."

My heart broke along with Eta's, the tearing sensation in my chest almost unbearable, and a tear slipped down both of our cheeks. And yet, Eta did not weep. There were no gulping, gasping sobs, the kind that causes hiccups and dripping noses. Just slow tears. Silent ones.

"We need to do something, Eta," the woman said. "We need to find a way to repel the Hunters, to protect our young."

Anger coursed through Eta's veins. "And what about the people we love?" Eta asked. "What about those? Not just the Coven, but the people we bring into our lives?"

Maren looked down, her old eyes sad. "It's part of being a witch, Eta. Especially during these times. And especially being women."

Eta said nothing, but I felt her anger, her heartache, the injustice of it all. The baby fretted at her breast, and she rocked again, her sad eyes on the forest.

Creak.
"Shhh ..."
Creak.

"The Coven—" Maren began.

"Not right now," Eta interrupted. "I love the Coven, and I will protect it. But for now, let me grieve."

Maren nodded, turning quietly, glancing over her shoulder only once before disappearing inside the cabin. Eta continued to stare into the woods.

The baby fussed, and Eta looked down.

"You look like your da," she whispered. "Shhh ... my sweet Mackenzie, my little Mac. You will be a strong woman one day. Beyond
tears."

The chair rocked. The baby fussed. Eta soothed.
Creak.
"Shhh ..."

The scene changed.

A full moon shone above a forest, and Eta was running, her hood flying back as she glanced periodically over her shoulder. Her hair gleamed in the moonlight. Twigs snapped as she stepped, and the wind moved through the leaves, howling along with predators I didn't care to put a name to. It wasn't cold here, but there was a slight chill in the air as if Spring was coming but Fall wasn't quite ready to let go.

And then, just as fast as she ran, Eta stopped, her breathing deep as she leaned over, her eyes on the ground. She was in a clearing, near a small creek, and the moon was large and clear above her, unimpeded by the forest's canopy. Eta stared up at it.

"Now. It all changes now," she whispered.

She leaned over and retrieved a stick from the forest floor, stripping it of any leaves before using it to draw a circle in the soil at her feet. From her dress, she pulled out four items and placed them in the North, East, South, and West quarters of the Circle. Most of the items, I couldn't make out, but one of them was a bowl, and she filled it quickly with water from the creek. She was invoking the elements. I knew this ritual well, and I hung back, my eyes on her black-handled athame as she pulled it from under her skirt and held it up.

In a language I didn't understand, she chanted, her body turning slowly, her face lifted.

"Lilith," she concluded.

I froze.

No!

Eta took the athame and sliced her palm. Blood fell to the ground.

My lips parted, and I started to protest, but a hand closed over my mouth, and I knew it was Luther's. I may not be able to see him, but he was with me in this vision, and his body was with mine in the present.

"No, Eta. Not this," I mouthed against Luther's palm.

But this was a vision, and I couldn't interfere. My heart broke. What had happened to Eta to make her think this was her only option?

Eta brought her fist into her chest and lowered her athame. The leaves within the forest stirred, and a dark cloud moved over the moon.

I shivered.

The clouds rolled away, and there within the forest glade, her pale body bathed in moonlight was Lilith, a black-haired svelte woman in a blood red dress with fair skin and red lips. Her eyes glowed, and when she smiled, her teeth were pointed.

Eta was suddenly unsure, her face scared. But it was too late. She had summoned the she-Demon, and there would be hell to pay.

"You summoned me, Witch?"

Lilith's voice was lyrical, beautiful, enchanting, and Eta watched in awe as the she-Demon moved around the Circle, her elegant glide effortless and intimidating.

Eta swallowed. "I-I need help."

Lilith's eyes took Eta in before she finally stepped toward the witch, her long, red fingernails coming up to run pointedly along Eta's white dress.

"White ... how *in*appropriate." Lilith laughed. "Tell me, dear, what is it you would have me do? What have you summoned me, one of the most powerful she-Demons in existence, to your petty little world for? Hmmmm ..."

Eta swallowed again. "My family, my Coven, and my lover ... all of them have been destroyed. All but a few of the Ayers witches remain. I am begging you to save the rest. To keep us safe."

Lilith grinned. "And you came to me? Why? Are you not capable of taking care of your own?"

Eta looked up, her jaw clenched.

"Ah," Lilith murmured. "So that's how it is. Who has wronged you so badly, Witch, that you would seek revenge?"

A lone tear slipped down Eta's cheeks. "The Hunters," she said fiercely. "*All* of them. We have suffered them too long. And ... a-and the people who killed my Mac."

Lilith laughed. "Oh, Witch, I have no issue with killing. If you want people dead, I can make that happen."

Lilith's eyes went cold, and her teeth lengthened, her pretty pale face transforming into the ferocious she-

Demon I knew she was. "But I don't take highly to being summoned, understand? I am not a Demon to be controlled. What you ask, so you shall have, but you will sacrifice much to get it."

Eta gasped. "No! No, please. I want only vengeance. For myself and for my people. I will give you anything of myself. My blood, my death even, but nothing else."

Lilith cocked her head, her eyes bright. "Foolish girl! You called me and offer only yourself! Oh no, Witch! I am worth much more than that. All of those involved in your lover's death will die. In fact, they die now, a mysterious illness taking them from this Earth, but your Hunters will live. Not all of them, but many will. I enjoy their work, you see. For, as a Demon, I find their intolerance and their methods of showing it interesting. *But,*" Lilith paused, her deadly face coming close to Eta's, "I *will* protect your family. In fact, your own daughter will protect your family.

For I will take my due. One witch of your line will call to the Hunters. Her power will draw them away from your Coven while a second witch of your line will belong to me. Your daughter's soul will add nicely to my collection."

Eta stood tall, her eyes full of fear. "No, it's not why I called you. I summoned you, and in my Circle, you are mine. I will offer you myself and nothing more. And you will do what I say."

Lilith's nails moved to Eta's neck. "Foolish, foolish girl. You think to control me? Let's sweeten the bargain then. From here on out, the souls of the Demon-cursed witches that belong to me will be tainted with evil. In each generation, the Demon-cursed among the Ayers will call to me, will summon me, will relish their angry power. And my collection of souls will grow. We both win then, sweet one. And yet, your Hunters will always be led astray. One Ayers witch will shed blood for the Hunters in each generation, and I will own the evil one."

Eta went to her knees. "No!" she cried. "No."

Lilith lifted Eta by her neck. "You called me, remember, witch? If you are so adamant your own blood should be spilled, then so be it."

And with that, Lilith ran one of her wickedly long red nails across Eta's neck.

I opened my mouth to scream and found myself restrained, Luther's mouth against my ear.

"It is Friday," he said. "January. You are in Salem, and it is ten thirty in the morning."

My breathing calmed, my vision cleared, and I was on the floor of Henry's parlor again. Luther was behind me, my back against his chest, and he released my mouth as Belle kneeled in front of us. I ignored her.

"Oh, Eta," I gasped. My forehead fell to my hands.

"Eta?" Belle asked. "The girl from your Scottish vision?"

I nodded. "She summoned Lilith."

It was all I could manage. My breathing was ragged, and I inhaled, concentrating once more on the clock in the hall. It helped to have a focal point when coming out of a vision. My mother had taught me that, had taught me to observe the world around me, to see it in ways other people might not.

Tick, tick, tick, said the clock.

And then, after a moment, "I'm supposed to be evil."

My words were low. Luther stood and moved from behind me, his hand lowered. I stared at his offered palm, but didn't take it.

"You know how I feel about evil," he said lightly.

I glared at him. "Bad is better for you. Not the rest of us."

He shrugged. "Well, I think it's safe to say something went wrong with this generation of Ayers witches. You're obviously not evil. Trouble maybe, but not evil."

I threw him another look as NeeCee made her way over to me, her strawberry blonde hair tied up, and her long-sleeve black tee wrinkled with little pieces of white fuzz on it.

She pushed up her glasses. "What happened in the vision?" she asked.

I told them, starting with the baby and ending with the ritual, my throat catching at the conclusion. I'd become Eta in those visions. I had felt her losses and her anger. Seeing her blood had torn me to pieces. Even if she had been the one to make the fatal Ayers mistake for so many of us. I'd felt her love for Mac, for her baby, for her family. Would I have made the same choice in her shoes?

"You think too much," Luther said from behind me.

NeeCee touched my shoulder. "So the Ayers witch who was supposed to die by the hands of the Hunters in the last generation still lives," NeeCee said. Her eyes came up to meet mine. "She chose to become a Hunter to save herself. By doing that, she has chosen to kill witches, to slaughter her own."

I knew instantly what NeeCee was saying, but it was Luther who spoke next.

He laughed. "So the hunted became the evil one."

Lucas pinched his nose. "I need a drink," he mumbled.

I arched a brow. "Do Angels drink?" I asked.

Lucas grinned. "I'm fallen, sweetheart. I have a lot of vices. If—"

"Hush!" Henry interrupted.

We all turned toward him. The seer was against the wall, his eyes on the picture window.

"I swear," he muttered. "I was sure—"

There was a loud sound from the yard beyond, and we all froze.

"Do you have any neighbors?" Belle asked, her voice low.

Henry nodded. "But I own seven acres of land, and my home is accessible to the woods.

The sound came again.

"Trouble," Henry breathed. "It can be nothing but trouble." His hand went to his blue jean pockets, retrieving an inhaler he immediately stuck in his mouth.

This time when the sound came, shadows moved along the walls. I wasn't facing the window, but I saw Luther's eyes narrow as he focused on something over my head.

His pupils reddened. "Get down!" he ordered just as the picture window on the side of the room imploded.

Chapter 18

Aunt Clara talks often of Hunters when we gather. One of the first lessons a witch learns is how to protect himself from a Hunter. There are protection spells that must be learned, even self-defense if there is time for it. But mainly, we are taught to avoid them. Clara looks often at NeeCee when she speaks. I wonder if it's because she thinks NeeCee is weak. As over protective as Clara is, I doubt NeeCee has anything to worry about.

~Monroe's Totally Wicked Book of Shadows~

My back went against the wall, my head slammed into the wood paneling. Black spots swam before my eyes.

"Damn it!" I heard Luther shout.

Little needle-like pin pricks exploded all over my body, and I moaned, my vision blurred. Figures moved in front of me, and I blinked hard.

Black masks. Shouting.

"Get up!" a voice said in my head. It wasn't mine. It was Luther's, and there was no way to fight him. Even with the pain, fighting him was out of the question. My body obeyed where my mind did not.

I knew when I stood, my hand going to the wall for support, that I was bleeding. There were small cuts everywhere, glass embedded in my skin, and I clenched my jaw as I fought to clear my vision.

In front of me, Luther was leaning over a masked intruder, his hand around the person's neck.

"You really think we'd let you find us first?" the masked figure asked. There was no doubt the intruder was a man.

Luther laughed. "You really think I didn't know you'd come?"

My head bobbed, and I blinked hard. When I opened my eyes again, Luther had the man against the wall, his mask removed. Behind him, Lucas had another man pinned to the floor.

And then, someone screamed. I stumbled.

"More of them!" Belle called out.

The man Luther was holding laughed. He was a bulky man, tall with long, braided dark hair. I stared at the braid. Hunters.

"NeeCee," I breathed, panicked. "Where's NeeCee?"

I tried to walk and went down on my knees. More needle-like pain, but this time I didn't cry out, this time I didn't care.

I crawled, glass digging into my hands, my knees.

"Monroe," a voice whispered, and I nearly cried in relief. NeeCee.

And then I looked up and froze.

Standing over Bernice was the blonde-haired woman from the cabin, the same one we'd seen in the bowl when we'd scryed, and in her hand, she clutched a gun. NeeCee was on her back on the floor, and she was shaking, her glasses knocked askew, her eyes on the gun's barrel.

I held up my hand, as if the gesture alone would make the woman stop.

"Maggie," I said softly.

The woman looked up, her hard, cold gaze moving to me. As soon as our eyes met, she grinned.

"Well, if it isn't Ellie Jacobs. Quite famous, you are, among the Hunters," Maggie said.

I could tell by the tone of her voice she was insane. I'd seen a look like that once in Dayton's aunt's eyes. At the time, she'd been controlled by a Demon. It made me thankful for Luther's presence in my head.

"We can talk about this, Maggie," I said.

I was suddenly one of those negotiators from all of the high drama cop shows on television, only this wasn't fictional, and I was about to lose NeeCee. And damned if every single *Law and Order* type speech didn't fly right out of my head.

Maggie's eyes narrowed, her gaze moving between me and Bernice. "Something's wrong," she said.

Her voice was hollow, her brows furrowed in confusion. Her gaze moved between us again, and I stiffened. *Calling powers.*

As the Hunter-cursed witch, Bernice was supposed to have calling powers that drew the Hunters away from the Ayers, but we'd swapped magic. It wasn't Bernice calling to Maggie now, it was me.

I kept my hand up. "Let her go. It's me you want," I said carefully.

Maggie shook her head, her eyes moving too quickly between us to be normal.

"No," she said slowly. "No, this isn't right."

I started to stand, and she waved her gun.

"You stay!" she ordered.

I froze. I may have power, but I was human in every other way. One shot, and I was as dead as any other mortal. My gaze locked on Maggie's even as Luther's voice infiltrated my mind.

"Don't move, Monroe!" he ordered.

I wanted to scowl, but didn't. What did he think I was going to do? Dance?

A gun went off somewhere in the house, and my body went numb. Who was dead? One of the Hunters? Or one of our own?

Maggie seemed unfazed. "This one here," she said, her gun gesturing at Bernice, "she was supposed to be the Hunted. I've been keeping tabs on her. And yet—"

"You were wrong, is all," I interjected. "People make mistakes, Maggie. Can't you feel it? That girl, *that* witch, is marked for Lilith. You wouldn't want to anger the she-Demon would you?"

Maggie started to lower her gun, real fear entering her eyes. And then, after a long and thoughtful moment, her gun rose again, the barrel aimed at my head.

I released the breath I'd been holding, my heart beating so hard within my chest I was sure it would explode long before a bullet could reach me. My eyes closed.

The gun went off.

Nothing. No searing pain, no blackness. *Nothing.*

I opened my eyes.

Maggie was on her back on the floor, her eyes on the Demon standing over her. Luther.

A few feet away was the gun. I crawled toward it.

"The big decision here at the moment," Luther said wryly. "is whether I kill you now or later."

Maggie's eyes widened, and Luther grinned. "I see you, Mother," he said, his tone low.

It was a freaky moment, gross even. If Lilith looked at me, would she see Luther in my head?

I shivered as my hand closed over Maggie's gun, the black metal cold in my palm. I lifted it.

"Do you even know how to use that?" Luther asked.

My gaze moved to him as I stood, the gun dangling at my side. To be honest, I knew nothing about weapons.

I shrugged. "It's a gun. You just point and shoot, right?" I asked.

Luther shot me a look as I approached him, which was funny really since he looked somewhat ridiculous with a booted foot on Maggie's chest.

I started to lift the gun, and Luther reached over, shaking his head as he grabbed me by the wrist, smoothly pulling the pistol out of my grip, his eyes locked on Maggie's.

"I'll take that," he said. "You with a gun doesn't seem like a very smart idea."

I raised my brows at his insult. "What? You actually have those?" I retorted. "Smart ideas, I mean."

Luther paused, flipping the gun before pressing it back into my palm.

"I've changed my mind. If you shoot yourself, you'll just be saving me the trouble."

Maggie watched us both, her eyes strangely alert.

"Oh, my God!" NeeCee said.

She had moved from the floor to the wall, her back pressed against the paneling, her eyes on the Hunter. My gaze followed hers.

Maggie's placid blue eyes, a trademark Ayers feature, had taken on a red hue, her pupils dilated. I swallowed a gasp. Luther did nothing.

"You dare interfere in my business, Son," Maggie said.

It wasn't the Hunter's voice that spoke, it was Lilith's, the she-Demon I'd seen in my vision of Eta.

"Oh, my God!" NeeCee said again.

Luther grinned. "Funny how we keep putting ourselves in this position, isn't it, Mother?" he asked.

Maggie's own lips turned up into a smile. I wanted to back away but didn't.

"The Ayers are mine, Thorne. I suggest you stay out of it," Lilith said.

There was a scuffle from behind me, and I turned just in time to see a masked Hunter barreling in my direction.

"Watch it!" Belle shouted. She was standing over a red-haired female, a stolen gun pointed at her head.

I didn't even attempt to use my own pistol. I really didn't know anything about guns. I threw it down instead, kicking it to the side as I ducked. The Hunter grabbed for me, and I moved under his arm, my foot coming down hard on the back of his knee before using my elbow against the back of his head.

The Hunter went down, and I used both mine and NeeCee's magic to hold him immobile.

I looked up to find Luther's eyes on me, and I shrugged sheepishly.

"Three brothers," I said simply. I'd had my fair share of wrestling opponents growing up, including a brother with martial arts training.

Luther eyes brightened, and I knew he was attempting not to smile.

"Monroe," Lilith's voice said suddenly. All of my humor fled as my gaze slid down to Maggie. "It's been a long time," the she-Demon added.

I kept my expression even. "Not long enough," I muttered.

Maggie laughed, the sound eerie because I knew it wasn't her voice. "I allowed you to get the upper hand on me once, Witch. I won't again. Your soul is mine."

Allowed? She'd allowed me?

Luther leaned over, his hand going to Maggie's chin, forcing her face in his direction. I winced at the way his fingers dug into her skin.

"It's time to let the Ayers go," he growled. "They've shed enough blood for you."

Maggie managed to smile despite Luther's grip, her red eyes glowing. "You really think so, Thorne? My son, the only one of my children whose abilities are so close to my own. You'd want to save them?"

Luther leaned close, his nose not far from Maggie's. "Search her, Mother, feel my presence in the Ayers. You're right. I am a lot like you. Don't mistake me for your other children. In the
end, I'm as evil as you are."

She laughed. "And yet you risk yourself for them now?"

The side of Luther's mouth lifted, the wry grin feral as his own eyes reddened. "She's been useful to me. You of all people know we never destroy what is useful to us."

I grit my teeth. Luther was right. I *was* useful to him, had been since I'd given him the amulet. Without me, he'd have his own possessive Demons to fight. Satan could possess any one of his Demons, and I'd kept him out of Luther.

"You don't want to fight me, Son," Lilith warned.

Luther stood, his head held high. "Oh, but I do. Prepare for war."

And with that, he lifted a hand and Maggie's eyes went wide before closing abruptly, her head lolling to the side.

"Did you kill her?" NeeCee asked, her voice small.

Luther looked up. "No."

It was all he said. No explanation. Nothing. Just "no". And when he turned to me and our eyes met, I realized something. Luther Craig really wasn't the good guy. We were all in bed with a villain. It suddenly wasn't about right or wrong. It was about which bad guy we were more willing to sell our soul to.

"You keep what you find useful, huh?" I asked, my voice void of all emotion, my eyes on Luther.

There was the sound of a body being dragged across the floor.

"Let's get them all tied up and save all the emotional stuff for later," Belle suggested in an attempt to diffuse the tension.

Behind me, Henry wheezed. "My window!" he whined. "Really!"

Lucas moved toward the seer, a Hunter dangling from his hands. "I'd worry more about the glass in your skin," the Angel said.

Henry paid him no attention. "My beautiful window. Do you even know how much money I put into this place?"

Luther's eyes were still glued to mine. "I've never pretended to be good," he told me. "The only one who pretended anything was you."

He moved past me then, and I sucked in a deep breath, my gaze going to NeeCee. She was still hugging the wall, her eyes wide. Blood oozed from a cut on her forehead. Smaller, less deep cuts peppered her arms. She looked at me, something akin to sympathy in her gaze.

Luther was right. he'd never pretended to be anything he wasn't. He'd marched onto the scene as a favor to his brother and had remained out of curiosity. I'd been okay with that, so why wasn't I now? And now that Luther knew the Ayers had once summoned his mother and had since bred women who would continue to summon her, why did he still stay? More curiosity? Or just because I was useful.

I moved toward NeeCee, my gaze on her cut. If being useful to Luther meant protecting her, did I really have a right to complain?

"My window!" Henry moaned again.

It was the last straw. Until now, I'd put up with a lot. I'd been okay being a favor. I'd put up with being possessed by a Demon. I'd relived my family history and bore Eta's scars, her heartache. And I'd listened to two Demons battle for the right to my soul. I'd become my worst fear. I'd lost all control.

"Screw your fucking window!"

And with that, I took NeeCee by the arm before brushing past everyone on our way up the stairs. No more! I wouldn't be used any more.

I wasn't known for being impractical, I wasn't known for throwing tantrums, and in my haste I missed when Maggie's head rolled again, her eyelids opening to reveal red eyes and a dangerous smile.

Chapter 19

I talked to Dayton today. It felt so good to hear her voice, but it was painful too. She wanted to know when or if I was coming back to Italy, but I'm still nowhere near learning why I am connected to Demons. All I have at the moment are dreams, visions, and empty theories. I hate this lonely feeling, this empty feeling that I'm not going to like what I discover about myself.

~Monroe's Totally Wicked Book of Shadows~

As soon as we were in the bedroom, I started throwing things.
"Damn!"
NeeCee sat heavily on the bed, her gaze distant.
"Damn!"
"Monroe," NeeCee whispered.
My hands went to the bedroom wall, and it was the first time I noticed all of the blood. The scratches and the blood. My forehead met my hands on the wall.
"I hurt," NeeCee said.
And now that she said it, I did too. My skin felt tight and raw. It stung and even burned in some places. I turned around, closing my eyes briefly before meeting her gaze.
"I'm sorry," I said. "I didn't mean to lose it like that."

NeeCee shook her head. "Don't apologize. It was bound to happen sometime. You certainly held out longer than I did."

I looked at my cousin, *really* looked at her. "What do you mean?"

She laughed. "Oh, I clocked out on you from the get go. Don't pretend I didn't, and don't think I'm not aware of the Demon in my head. I knew when Luther possessed me. Your power wouldn't let me ignore it. It just seemed easier to let him control me." NeeCee's eyes teared up. "I guess that makes me weak.

I moved to her, my hands taking hers. She winced, and I tried not to do the same. Glass cuts were like paper cuts. They might not always look terrible, but they hurt hella bad.

"Don't do that to yourself, NeeCee. You aren't weak. You never have been. Honestly, you're smart, you're pretty, and you have way more gumption than you think you do. Sometimes it takes more guts to let people lead you, than it does to lead. I know you. You'd go along with it as long as it was for your own good, but you would have fought if it wasn't. Don't sell yourself short. You're an Ayers."

NeeCee snorted. "A damn lot of good that has done us."

I laughed because, really, there wasn't anything else I could do.

"We have some good family too," I said. "Our parents for one." My thoughts went to Mac. "And others."

NeeCee started picking at the glass in her arms, and I did the same, my teeth clenched.

"What do we do now?" NeeCee asked.

I glanced at her, my eyes going to a piece of glass she was holding in her hands. An idea blossomed in my head. The glass wasn't quartz, but ...

"NeeCee," I said carefully.

She looked at me. "Yeah."

I stood and moved over to a clear glass vase I'd noticed when I'd awoken to find Luther leaning over me on the bed, the grimoire under my head.

I froze. The grimoire! It was downstairs. I cringed at the thought of going after it.

"Monroe," NeeCee said.

I shook myself. The grimoire was the least of our problems at the moment.

"Do you trust me?" I asked NeeCee as I lifted the vase.

NeeCee swallowed. "You know I do," she said slowly.

I dropped the vase, and it shattered on the floor. I took two large shards and brought them over to the bed before lifting NeeCee's hand.

"Then repeat after me," I instructed.

I took one of the shards and reopened one of NeeCee's cuts.

She cried out. "Monroe!"

"Just trust me," I repeated.

I smeared both glass shards with her blood and then handed them to her. "Blood on glass ..."

NeeCee didn't say anything, and I shook her. "Say it!"

NeeCee jumped but hastily repeated the lines.

I stared into her eyes. "Blood on glass, repel my enemy, possession pass, control remain with me, this I say, so let it be."

NeeCee repeated the chant, her eyes wide with fear and hope as the shards brightened and took on a bluish-white glow before fading. Her blood was gone, absorbed into the glass.

"Was that what I think it was?" Bernice whispered.

I nodded. "It's the same spell I did on the quartz when I created the amulets. The only change is the word quartz to glass. Now ..." I looked around the room and grabbed one of the pillows off of the bed, stripping the white pillowcase off of it. "Now we make them wearable."

I used an extra piece of glass to rip the pillowcases, wrapping the resulting fabric around the outside of the spelled glass shards.

NeeCee jumped up. "The blinds! We can use the cords from the window blinds to tie them around our necks."

I smiled. "That's my girl."

NeeCee tried giving me a stern look but ended up laughing instead.

I grinned wider as she cut down the blind cord before handing me a good piece of it. "It's nice to feel empowered, isn't it?" I asked.

Neither one of us said anything as we knotted a piece of cord around the fabric-wrapped glass, and then used the remaining cord to fasten it around our necks.

Our eyes met.

"Blessed be," we whispered simultaneously.

As soon as I dropped the glass to my shirt, I felt the difference. My head was suddenly lighter. Empty.

NeeCee laughed again. "It worked, Monroe. I still feel the Demon, but he's not inside any more!"

I grinned. "As long as you have my power, you'll feel him, but you're right, he's not possessing us now."

She sat down, her hands coming to mine, her eyes turning serious. "We're it, Monroe. We're this generation's sacrifice."

My eyes searched hers. "Yes ... yes, we are. But we're also the first generation of Ayers that didn't call to Lilith." I gripped her hands. "And even if she was summoned by the Hunter, we can fight this. We both don't have to die."

The tone of my voice was obvious, and Bernice's eyes widened. "What are you saying, Monroe?"

I leaned forward. "I'm saying that if Lilith's sacrifices must be met, there is still a Hunter-cursed Ayers who could die in your place."

NeeCee gasped. "Monroe! You wouldn't!"

"I won't," I agreed. "I won't if I don't have to."

"Monroe," NeeCee whispered.

I shook my head. "No, NeeCee. I won't make any promises. I'd do anything for my family. You are family."

NeeCee sat up, her head falling to her chin.

"I love you, Roe," she said.

I grinned. "Right back at ya!"

There was a knock at the door, and I dropped NeeCee's hands, my back straight as I turned to face it.

NeeCee gasped. "It's a Demon. The shock is not as strong with the amulet, but it's still a Demon."

I scowled. "I figured it wouldn't take Luther long once we kicked him out of our heads." I stood. "Not now, Luther!" I called out.

NeeCee stood next to me, a frown on her face.

"Monroe," she whispered. "Something's wrong."

I stiffened, my eyes on the door.

"Don't tell me what I think you're going to tell me, NeeCee."

A small sob escaped her, and I knew she'd been overcome with fear.

I moved in front of her. "NeeCee ..."

She sobbed again. "I don't think it's Luther," she whispered.

The knock came again.

I stepped forward, my hand going to the amulet, my eyes narrowed, my lips moving quietly. The protection spell was a simple one, and it calmed Bernice as it wrapped around us, but if it was who I thought it was, it wasn't going to do a damn bit of good.

NeeCee's hand went to my sweatshirt, her fingers clenching the fabric just as the door suddenly swung open.

NeeCee screamed.

Chapter 20

I stood at the railing facing the river today, and when I was sure the coast was clear, I climbed on top of it. It probably wasn't the smartest thing in the world to do, but I needed a closer connection to the Goddess than I could get from the ground. It was like flying. The wind was strong, so I stood carefully, without moving until I felt confident enough to close my eyes, but when my lids finally fluttered closed, I was flying. I was part of the wind, part of the air. I'm not an elemental witch, so I know I don't have a particular talent for an individual element, but water is reassuring right now. With all of the dreams I'm having of fire, water is keeping me sane.

~Monroe's Totally Wicked Book of Shadows~

The woman on the other side of the door wasn't Maggie anymore. It was a wild shell of a woman, her blonde-braided hair tangled and sticking up haphazardly around her head. Her skin looked sickly, almost yellow, and the grin on her face was manipulated, her lips way too wide to be real. Her eyes were blood red.

NeeCee was still screaming, the shriek broken intermittently by sobs, and I reached behind me to grab her hand. She calmed but barely.

"Miss me?" Lilith's voice asked.

NeeCee hiccupped.

I stayed in front of Bernice. "What do you want, Demon?" I asked.

Maggie's body moved into the room, her movements graceful. The elegance was odd when mixed with the Hunter's appearance.

"Let's see," Lilith said. "Your family owes me, and I'm long past due getting paid."

She was close enough now, I could make out Maggie's pupils. The visionary in me reared its ugly head, and I saw past the Demon now occupying Maggie's body to the woman beneath. Below all of the red, there was regret and fear in her eyes. I might not like Maggie very much right now, but I couldn't hate her. She had been a Hunter-cursed Ayers, and she'd done the only thing she knew to survive. Join the ranks of the people sent to kill her. It was a choice she should never have had to make.

"Where are the others?" I asked.

It wasn't humanly possible for Maggie's grin to get any wider, but it did. "I'm Lilith, Witch. They were fools to think they could overcome me. And now the fun part ..." she gestured at the bedroom window. "Tonight, in the Salem Woods, you will sacrifice them all. Every last one of them, except the captured Hunters. They are gone. I let them go and sent them away."

I froze, and Lilith laughed. "That's right. You think that petty little amulet will keep me from you, Monroe, but you're wrong. I created you. I created your magic, your tie to Demons, and I will have your soul. The rest is simply an added bonus. The amulet can protect you from all Demons but me. I know you know I'm right. Your family has shed blood for me, Monroe. It's my power, your connection to me, that makes your little amulet work in the first place."

Maggie snapped her fingers.

"But first," Lilith's voice said. "Let's fix one pesky little problem."

Maggie's hand lifted, and I almost went down on my knees. NeeCee gasped.

"Monroe!" NeeCee called out.

I couldn't answer her. The electricity that suddenly lit up my body was too much, and I stumbled. Bernice caught me, her presence at my back keeping me on my feet, steady.

"I've got you," NeeCee said, the determination in her voice obvious. When it came to family, she did have courage.

The electric tingles died down, but they didn't go away. My magic was back, and NeeCee's powers were gone. Somehow Lilith had reversed the power swap spell.

I clung even harder to the amulet, one finger slipping beneath the fabric I'd wrapped around the glass. It pierced my skin, and I chanted what I'd made Bernice chant before. Lilith said the amulet wouldn't work against her, but I could still hold out hope.

Maggie stepped toward us, her body wavering as it neared mine.

"I'll be going now," Lilith said. "But be ready, Witch. Tonight I come for you, and there will be no way to stop it. Tell my son this is a war even he can't win. Thorns are only good if they come attached to a rose."

And with that, Maggie's body went limp, falling flat on her face at my feet. NeeCee screamed again.

I leaned down, my hand going to Maggie's pulse.

"Is she dead?" Bernice asked.

I closed my eyes, my heart heavy. I felt nothing in Maggie's wrist. Lilith had taken away any chance I had at saving Bernice. I'm not sure I could have actually brought myself to take someone's life, but it had still been an option. Now, Lilith had taken Maggie's spirit and left Bernice and I the only two Ayers witches left to meet her due.

I looked up at Bernice. "She's gone."

NeeCee sobbed.

I stood and took her hand. "Come on, NeeCee. Stay strong. We need to find out what happened to the others."

She nodded, and we raced out of the bedroom, our feet thundering on the stairwell. I heard the clock before I saw the parlor. *Tick, tick, tick.*

I slowed as the edge of the pool table came into view.

"Belle," NeeCee whisper-yelled, and I shushed her.

"It won't matter," a voice said from behind us. "They won't hear you."

NeeCee shrieked, and I inhaled sharply, my panic controlled simply by the fact that I knew the voice. I'd know it anywhere.

I turned. "What happened?"

Luther pushed away from the wall he was leaning against, his eyes red as he moved toward us.

"I see you figured out a way to make an amulet even before your powers were returned," he said.

I stared at him. "What happened?" I repeated.

Luther looked over my head. "I underestimated her," he said simply. "My mother has gotten stronger since I faced her last. I won't make that mistake again."

I reached out and fisted my hand in Luther's shirt. His eyes moved down to mine.

"Where are they?" I asked.

"Taken," Luther answered.

I think I would have sagged if I hadn't been holding on to Luther's shirt.

"Lilith came to us," I said quietly. "In Maggie's body. She said ... she said I'm supposed to sacrifice them all tonight."

Luther didn't speak, and I went on my toes, my face as close to his as I could get.

"Be honest with me, Demon. Can she posses me? Even with the amulet, can she possess me and make me kill?"

Luther's eyes met mine. "Yes."

I sagged, my eyes going back to the parlor. It was cold inside the house now, and I could hear the wind as it came through the broken window beyond. Sunlight glinted on scattered glass, and the pages of an open book fluttered as the breeze caught it.

My eyes widened. "The grimoire!"

I released Luther and moved toward the book. I didn't have to look to know he followed.

"I'm an Ayers," I said as I knelt, my hands going to the book that had been in our family for centuries. "In the beginning, we were strong witches with our destinies our own." I picked up the grimoire. "I won't be ruled."

Luther's hand found my shoulder. "Good," he said, kneeling just enough to grasp me by the waist. He helped me up. "Then be bad for once, Monroe." My gaze met his, and he leaned forward. "You can't be good and win a battle with Lilith."

My face was entirely too close to his. "You aren't good, and it looks like she beat you."

I could see Luther's bicep tighten, and I knew he was fisting his hand.

"No one is infallible, Monroe. The she-Demon gave birth to me. In the long run, she created me. It doesn't mean she's indestructible, but she can damn sure surprise me. Point one for her. It's all I'm willing to let her have."

I searched his eyes. "And so you plan to defeat her?" I asked. "What does that mean for me and Bernice?"

Luther's hand tightened on my waist. "You were right when you told me I'm not like my brother. I'm not anything like Marcas. I have no plans to usurp my way into power, and I have no desire to be anything other than the Demon I was born to be."

I was confused. "Then you don't plan to fight her?" I asked.

Luther laughed. "Oh no, I most definitely plan to fight her. For one, I hate to lose."

"For one?" I whispered.

Luther grinned. "And for the other, I happen to like you."

My eyes narrowed. "And that means something to a Demon who claims he isn't good."

"Of course it does," another voice cut in.

My head shot up. Lucas. Of course! If anyone could avoid Lilith's clutches, it would be him. The fallen Angel was near the stairwell, his hand on the banister. He looked tired, if that were even possible. Whatever had happened
downstairs, Lucas and Luther had put up one Hell of a fight.

My eyes met Lucas'. "And how does liking me mean anything?" I asked.

Lucas' gaze went from mine to Luther's. "Because passion, Monroe, can mean as much to a Demon as hate."

My eyes shot back to Luther's. The Demon leaned close and winked. "Don't get too close, Witch. I burn."

Chapter 21

I dream, and I am consumed by fire.

~Monroe's Totally Wicked Book of Shadows~

It was two p.m., and Luther had left. Where he went was beyond me, and I showered and changed for the second time that day before returning downstairs with the grimoire under my arm, my body stiff from small cuts. I'd only looked at my face once in the bathroom mirror and immediately looked away. It had been as peppered with small cuts as my arms.

In a fresh, plain black sweatshirt and another pair of jeans, I met Bernice at the bottom of the stairs, her own clothes fresh and her hair damp. I was out of clothes. Another day here, and I'd need to borrow Henry's washer and dryer.

Lucas was standing near the grandfather clock, his eyes on the stairs, on us.

My gaze met his. "What happened after Bernice and I went upstairs earlier?" I asked.

I expected more of a straight answer from Lucas than I did Luther. The fallen Angel walked toward me, his face unreadable. He really was handsome.

"Lilith faced off against Luther. It was quite a fight. A lot of power passed between them. I did what I could, but even together, it wasn't enough. Funny thing is,

Lilith used Maggie's body. Defeating her should have been easy. When a Demon fights through possession, their power should be weaker."

I stared at him. "You forget something, Lucas," I said. "Maggie was a witch. She had her own powers, and if Maggie had summoned the Demon, then Lilith would have had access to both the witch's powers and her own."

Bernice snorted. "I think witches are highly underestimated."

I agreed.

Lucas looked away. "Even so, Luther and I should have held her back."

Lucas stepped away from us, moving silently down the hallway, and Bernice and I followed.

"You think she's hiding something?" I asked.

Lucas stopped inside of a large kitchen with stainless steel appliances and brick accents. A large wine rack sat against the wall, and copper pots hung over a stone island with wrought-iron, padded bar stools.

"Lilith managed to overcome both Luther and I together," Lucas said, turning to face me, one hand against the kitchen island. NeeCee moved to one of the bar stools. "She overcame *both* of us. That takes a lot of power. And then she took Belle and Henry hostage only to claim they are sacrifices for you. Yes, I think she's hiding something, and I don't like it."

Lucas looked at the refrigerator. "You should eat. Both of you."

I grew green at the gills just thinking about food, but Lucas was right. It wouldn't do for us to get weak now. I laid the grimoire on the bar before moving to the fridge. I couldn't shake Lilith's words from the bedroom earlier out of my head. *Tell my son this is a war even he can't win. Thorns are only good if they come attached to a rose.*

"Thorns are only good if they come attached to a rose," I whispered as I located some cold cut meats and cheese while NeeCee searched the kitchen for bread.

"Did you say something?" NeeCee asked.

She'd found the bread and had placed a few slices on two plates she'd pulled from the cabinet.

I shook my head. "No, it's nothing."

We ate in silence after that, my eyes going to Lucas where he stood now at a small kitchen window, his hands behind his back. *She's hiding something,* he'd said. I wasn't sure there was much for Lilith to hide. She owned the Ayers. We'd shed blood for her. Was it Lilith hiding something or Luther?

Lucas turned suddenly, his eyes going to mine. "You should rest now," he said.

I gaped at him. "Rest? Are we really supposed to wait for Lilith to come and take me away?"

Lucas didn't move. "Until we know what she has in mind, there is nothing else we can do."

I stared at him a moment, my gaze full of disbelief, before I finally picked up the grimoire and nodded at Bernice. She slid off of her bar stool and moved out of the room. I wasn't far behind her. At the kitchen's entrance, I stopped.

"Are we waiting now because that's what Luther wants?" I asked. Lucas didn't answer, and I looked over my shoulder. "It is, isn't it? I thought once that you hated him. Why do you follow him now?"

Lucas sighed before running a hand through his hair, his eyes closing a moment before they met mine again.

"Honestly?" he asked. "Because this war with Lilith and her children has been long past due. Luther may have his flaws, but I've learned something about the

Craig brothers over the past couple of human years." I held my breath as Lucas took a step forward, his eyes hard. "They have a really skewered sense of justice, but it's there all the same. The only ones who can truly defeat Lilith are her own children. Luther has always been most like her both in personality and in power. Your family made the ultimate mistake, Witch. They called on Lilith. I'm not sure you truly understand what that means."

My arms tightened on the grimoire. "And what does it mean, then?" I asked.

Lucas' eyes were sad. "Your family called on a Demon. It forfeited any right to protection you have from Heaven." His gaze moved from NeeCee to me. "And in *this* generation, Maggie called on Lilith. You and Bernice belong to the she-Demon now. You are, by right, the sacrifice Lilith claims for the protection she believes she has gifted your family all of these years."

"What are you saying?" I whispered.

Lucas was in front of me now, his blue eyes locked on mine. "Your family sold a soul to Lilith by summoning her. Whatever soul she pleases. It means that by helping you, all of us are breaking the rules. It means that right now, as much as we all hate to admit it, Luther is your best chance."

And with that, the Angel walked away, leaving me standing, my heart sinking.

Chapter 22

I often find myself reliving the kiss the Demon Luther gave me in exchange for an amulet. It was a harsh kiss, possessive despite the fact we know nothing about each other. I've had kisses before. I've had relationships before, one of them serious. It lasted over a year. So why do I keep remembering a kiss from a near stranger?

~Monroe's Totally Wicked Book of Shadows~

Two hours later, and I found myself sitting in a dark living room downstairs, my eyes on a flat widescreen television with an old black and white film off of Turner Classic Movies throwing bright flashes of light against the room's wine-colored walls. The black suede couch I sat on was thick and soft, and I sank into the cushions, my gaze going from the muted television to the glass coffee table in front of me. The grimoire.

"Feeling hopeless?" a voice asked.

I closed my eyes. "And if I am?"

The couch cushion next to me shifted as Luther sat down. "And you accused Demons of feeling lonely and afraid," he said snidely.

I opened my eyes. "Aren't you?"

Luther laughed. "*I'm* not. You're only what you allow yourself to be."

I shrugged one shoulder. "Then I'm allowing myself to feel hopeless."

"Liar," Luther accused, his mouth turned up into a grin. "I've been inside your head, remember? You don't give yourself much room to feel hopeless."

I was finding it hard not to grin at him. Luther had that effect. I could be downright pissed at him, and he'd still make me smile.

Luther's eyes went to the television, and then back to me. "Old Hollywood. I dated an actress back then," he said with a wink. "Seems more glamorous on the screen than it actually was."

I scowled. "Don't mess with my delusion."

His dark eyes searched my face. "It's kind of hard to watch a movie if you can't hear it."

I had my feet tucked underneath me, and I shifted, letting my toes touch the wood floor. Anger swept through me.

"It's more for comfort," I said, my eyes narrowed on his face. "I'm having a hard time resting when Belle and Henry are suffering God knows what with your mother."

Luther's eyes moved away from my face and down to my lap. I was ringing my hands, not so much out of fear as anxiety. He started to cover my hands with his, and I pulled away.

"Lilith won't hurt them," Luther promised. "If anything, she will wine and dine them. She gets a kind of perverted satisfaction out of giving people the things they enjoy most out of life before killing them."

That didn't make me feel any better.

I drew in a deep breath. "What if I just offered her my soul? Would she let them all go then, including Bernice?"

Luther sat up abruptly, his fingers going to my chin. He gripped it painfully, forcing me to look him in the face.

"You don't know what you'd be offering, Witch," he growled. "If you think being a Demon is such an awful life, you don't want to be the eternal servant of one. You understand?"

His eyes moved back and forth, and I watched, fascinated as his eyes bled from forest green to red and back again. He leaned in, and I inhaled. Luther smelled like nothing I'd ever smelled before. Like sin should smell. Like chocolate tasted as it melted on the tongue. Like a fire would smell without the smoke.

"I liked it better when I was inside your head," he murmured.

I placed my hand on his, tugging on it as I continued to look at him. Baseball caps. He collected baseball caps. I kept repeating that over and over in my head.

"Why are you so willing to fight your mother for my soul?" I asked him. "You don't
know me. Not really. You could be inside my head for years, and you still wouldn't know everything. So I gave you an amulet once that kept Lucifer out of your head? And? Is that why you're doing this? Really?"

Luther let me pull his hand away, but he immediately trapped my fingers in his, his eyes gleaming.

"Maybe I like the idea of beating my mother," he said.

I snorted. "When this first started, we had no idea your mother was involved. Be honest with me."

Luther stared at our fingers. "I'm fascinated by you."

His answer surprised me, and I fought to pull away from him.

"That's it?" I asked. "Your *fascinated* with me?" I laughed. "You would fight your mother for my soul out of fascination?"

Luther shrugged. "Look at me," he said, and I did. "I live my life out of want rather than need. If I want something, I take it. It's the truth. I don't try to hide it. But I'm only half-Demon, Monroe. I do have the tendency to care about people. I don't like it. Hell, I hate it, but it's there. My brother, for one. For him, I would do much. I owe my brother and your friend, Dayton, a lot. I like you. I'm fascinated by you. And I hate my mother. That's enough for me. If you are looking for something deeper, you won't find it."

His gaze had me hypnotized. "I wasn't looking for anything deeper," I argued.

Luther brows rose. "Weren't you? Isn't that what women do? Try to change what they believe is bad?"

I shook my head again. "You can't change what doesn't want to be changed."

Luther grinned. "Exactly."

I looked at Luther, and like I did with Bernice earlier, I *really* looked at him, at his cocky grin, at his muscled body and black t-shirt, at the way he held his shoulders back with a confidence most people never find. He was comfortable with himself. He was mischievous, even bad at times, but he was honorable enough to repay those he owed. He didn't pretend to care about people, but he didn't necessarily destroy people either. I certainly didn't want to be his enemy. He genuinely liked who he was, and there was something sexy about that.

The thought surprised me, and I gazed at him openly. "I wouldn't want you to change."

The words slipped out, and I couldn't have taken them back even if I wanted to.

Luther eyes narrowed. "What?"

I started to get up, and Luther stopped me.

"What did you say?" he asked.

"Nothing," I said hastily. "I didn't say anything."

I tried once more to move, but Luther's grip on me was firm, unrelenting.

"Then say *nothing* again," he ordered.

I just managed not to snort. "You're not in my head anymore, Luther. You can't make me do anything."

His hand tightened on my arm. "Say it," he repeated.

His demanding voice surprised me, and I looked at him again, my eyes searching his fierce expression. What I saw in his gaze surprised me.

"I said I wouldn't want you to change," I said slowly, quietly.

Luther released me, and I rubbed my arm as he reached out and touched my hair. It was down now, and it swung against my glass-scarred cheeks. Memories of my past with Luther bombarded me. The mischievous Luther. Even Dayton had warned me away from him in her own way. Why? Because he was okay being who he was?

"You should really take your own advice, Witch," Luther said suddenly. "Quit trying so hard to change."

My eyes widened. I wasn't trying to change, was I?

Luther leaned in. "You don't have to pretend to live in the past all the time, Monroe."

I had just opened my mouth to protest when an electric shock went through my body, and it wasn't from Luther. I pushed him away and braced myself. Luther stiffened next to me, his teeth clenched.

"Whatever you do," Luther said, just as Lilith's terrifying laughter filled the living room, "fight like hell."

On the television, a laughing June Allyson was being being kissed by a gallant Van Johnson.

Chapter 23

When I was ten, I fell off a roof because I thought I could fly on a broomstick. In my own defense, I knew my mother was a witch, and we had been watching a lot of Hocus Pocus because it was almost Halloween. Bette Midler, Kathy Najimy, and Sarah Jessica Parker played commercialized witches, what society liked to think witches were like, but I still thought they were kind of cool. I even went around making sucking noises around Conor and Dayton in an attempt to suck out their life forces. That lasted a day before Conor poured red kool-aid on my hair. It took a week for my hair to look blonde again. It was the only time in my life I've ever thought being an evil witch would be cool.

~Monroe's Totally Wicked Book of Shadows~

"Hello, Monroe," Lilith crooned as she entered the room.

I grabbed my head as pain exploded behind my eyes. "Ahhhhhh!"

Lilith laughed. "Hurts doesn't it?"

Beside me, Luther's hand touched my arm, and the pain lessened. It didn't go away, but it lessened. The makeshift amulet around my neck was so bright, it was blinding. Even through the fabric.

"You're becoming a nuisance, Son," Lilith said sweetly.

Luther stood. "Wonderful. Nothing makes me happier."

Lilith's eyes moved to Luther's. "I've come to take my due. You know as well as I do, you can't stop me. Her soul is mine."

Luther held his hands up. "I'm not trying to stop you, Mother. I wouldn't dream of it."

The pain in my head intensified, and I slid from the couch to the floor, my hand grabbing instinctively for the grimoire. I clutched it, my teeth grinding together.

"Come!" Lilith's voice ordered in my head, and I could feel sweat break out on my forehead as my legs started to move of their own accord. I pushed them down.

"No!"

I hadn't realized I'd said the word aloud until Lilith laughed.

"Cute," she said. "You think you can best me, Witch. I'm impressed. I think your soul is going to be the jewel in my collection."

"Come!" her voice shouted, and my arms and legs began to shake even as they moved. I fought harder, my teeth grinding painfully with each step. I was pretty sure I resembled something from a bad B-rated zombie film, but jerky was better than controlled.

The amulet began to glow so brightly, it burned.

Lilith cursed.

"That damned necklace!" she said, her body moving toward me.

It was the first time I'd really gotten a good look at the she-Demon since I'd seen her in the vision with Eta, and it terrified me. Her black hair blew around her face, an invisible wind lifting it around her head, twisting and turning the strands until it resembled angry snakes.

Her blood red lips sneered at me, her eyes gleaming, fiery jewels as she approached me, her sharp, scarlet nails lifting so quickly, I wasn't prepared for the *snap* as the blinds cord around my neck came apart. The shard of glass attached to it went to the floor and shattered.

I whimpered as her hand came to my face. "Come, Monroe," she ordered.

And I followed because, really, there was nothing else I could do. My vision blurred. I was in the living room one moment, and then the hall. Maybe?

I shook my head, but it didn't help.

"All is well. Be calm." Lilith's voice said in my head, and I went limp.

Once, I thought I saw Lucas step up to Luther, his face angry, but I couldn't be sure.

"Lilith!" Lucas called, but Luther placed a hand on the Angel's shoulder.

"No," Luther said, his angry red eyes on his mother. "Not yet, Angel. We bide our time."

Lilith laughed at the two of them, the sound ripping through my frame. I'm pretty sure I screamed.

And then there was crying.

NeeCee!

I fought Lilith's iron control over my mind, kicking and screaming until my lungs were on fire and my head felt like it was going to explode.

"Stop this, Witch!" Lilith ordered, and once again, I grew still.

Was this how Maggie felt before she died? Like a puppet with a ventriloquist's hand up her back, controlling her every move.

I think I said *please*, but it may have been a figment of my imagination.

"Monroe!" someone shouted. NeeCee.

Tears slid down my cheeks. Eternity as a puppet.

My bare feet were moving through grass now, and it was damp outside. Twigs caught at my toes, pine

needles and acorns eating into my flesh, and I was tired.
"Walk!"

The order was harsh, and my feet sped up of their own accord, my teeth grinding as pain went through my soles. I was stepping on stone and dirt and pine cones.

"Please!" I begged.

This time, I was pretty sure the words came from me. I didn't slow.

"No," Lilith cackled. "We have a lot to do tonight, Monroe. Be prepared. Tonight is going to change your life forever."

Forever.

The word echoed throughout my head.

Forever.

Over and over.

Forever.

Distantly, I realized I was still holding the Ayers grimoire in my hands, my fingers pressing into it so tightly, they were leaving impressions in the cover. I waited for it to fall away from me, for Lilith's control to make me drop it. But it stayed in my arms, secure, warm. So many Ayers witches. So many of their souls trapped now by Lilith. I could almost feel them, their pain as fresh as mine.

I lifted my head. I was a witch. I was an *Ayers* witch! I could fight her. I could! *Fight like hell*, Luther had said. I almost laughed at the irony.

My vision cleared.

I was in the forest, and I was freezing. I had on my sweatshirt and blue jeans, but with my feet bare, I was a block of ice. My mother had always joked that as long as she kept my feet warm, the rest of me would follow.

I thought of her now. My mother. My teeth were chattering, my feet so cold they were painful, the throbbing so intense it made me cry. I hated crying.

"Stop!" Lilith ordered, and I froze.

We were in a clearing, and the sky above it was dark blue, not quite navy, but close. A full moon was rising. I wasn't sure how much time had passed since Lilith had ordered me to follow her, but it was obvious by the sky, it had been a couple of hours.

"Welcome to your eternity," Lilith said, one red-clawed hand indicating the trees on the edge of the clearing.

There, tied to three different tree trunks, was Belle, Henry, and Bernice, their mouths gagged, and their eyes wide, terrified. Bernice's cheeks glistened, and I knew she was crying.

"No," I whispered.

Lilith was suddenly behind me, her breath on my neck, and my heart went to my throat.

"Oh yes, Monroe," she said, her hands guiding my head to the middle of the clearing.

I swallowed a sob. On the ground, there lay four small brown bags and a black-handled athame. I'd seen them before. They belonged to Eta.

"No," I said again.

Lilith smiled. "Oh, it's been years since I have felt this energetic about something," she said. "Just look at it all! Isn't it beautiful?"

It wasn't beautiful. It was horrible!

I wanted to cover my face with my hands, but I wasn't willing to drop the grimoire. Why? I had no idea. I was beginning to hate the book,
and yet something about it wouldn't let me let it go.

Lilith noticed me clutching it, and she tapped the cover with her nails.

"So many of your family's stories. Such private moments. Tell me, Witch, do you have your own book of shadows?"

The muscles in my jaw moved as I clenched it, my eyes straight ahead.

Lilith laughed. She was doing a lot of laughing.

"Are you ready to meet your destiny?" she asked.

The anger that unfurled in my belly warmed me, and I looked at her and hoped like hell my blue eyes were shining.

"This is not my destiny."

"Oh we'll see about that," Lilith answered me.

The trees behind us stirred, the movement too strong to be the wind.

Lilith looked up. "Come to watch?" she asked.

I didn't have to look behind me to know who it was. I felt the electrical energy all the way to my toes.

"What?" Luther asked. "You of all people know how much I like front row seats. I even saved a few spots for some of your favorite people."

His words made me look up, my eyes going to the forest beyond. Luther stepped from the foliage, Lucas on his heels.

My body began to tingle, the energy familiar.

"Hello, Mother," another male voice said.

Out of the trees stepped Marcas Craig, the large, black-haired hybrid king of the Outer Levels of Hell, and with him was my best friend, Dayton Blainey. Both of their eyes glowed red.

Chapter 24

Mom used to tell me I was an obstinate child. It wasn't that I was bad, I was just stubborn. I was a boss, always ordering my three older brothers around as if they were little toy soldiers rather than big, growing young men. I was, in all actuality, a complete and utter control freak.

~Monroe's Totally Wicked Book of Shadows~

Relief, hope, and joy had just begun to fill my veins when my body was suddenly lifted into the air and slammed against a tree on the opposite side of the clearing.

"Monroe!" Dayton screamed.

I crumpled to the ground, the grimoire falling from my grip.

"Stay low!" Lilith ordered, and I went down on my stomach, my cheek against the grass.

I could just make out a group of small insects marching in front of my eyes as a tear slid down my cheek onto the soil below my face. Lilith was going to kill me. She was going to break my body until there was nothing left to put together the same way she'd done to Maggie. Even now, I could feel the blood seeping through my sweatshirt where my side had gone into the tree, the skin scraped by the bark.

"What business do you have here, Marcas?" Lilith asked.

The hybrid king said nothing at first, and I managed to roll my head just enough to make out the group opposite me. Marcas was perusing the clearing, his eyes raking the victims tied to the trees before they made their way to me.

"Monroe," a male voice said in my head.

Lilith roared, one fist lifted into the air.

"No!" she screamed, her finger pointed at Marcas. "This one is mine. You understand me? Mine! And she is mine by right. As a king of Hell, you know that."

Marcas' head lifted, his gaze going to his mother.

"Then release the ones who owe you nothing. The seer and the black-haired witch."

I took deep breaths through my nose, my side hurting so badly, I began to wonder if I'd broken a rib. My fingers dug into the damp soil.

Lilith's head rose. "The seer. He can go, but the others die."

The she-Demon's voice filled my head, and I rolled onto my back, my hands going over my ears as I screamed. It wasn't a natural scream. I knew it before it even exited my mouth. It was a desperate one, the kind you find yourself wanting to scream in the middle of a nightmare right before you freeze. Only I didn't freeze, I screamed, and I fought, my side on fire as I dug my fingers and toes into the ground.

Her voice entered my head again, and I sobbed as I found myself getting onto my knees, my body propelling itself forward slowly. And I fought, digging my toes and fingers into the ground with each forward creep until the pads of my fingers began to bleed, and my toes began to cramp.

And still her words persisted. Awful, *horrible* words.

"Stop this!" I heard Dayton yell.

Lilith laughed. I was getting really, really sick of her laugh.

"Your lover here may not have told you, dear, but he can't stop me. When a Demon is summoned, sacrifices must be met."

"Luther!" Dayton begged.

Nothing. No sound. No protests.

My gaze went to Luther's as I crawled, his steady, confident face completely unreadable. But his eyes, they said so many things he was never willing to say.

"Whatever you do," he'd told me at Henry's house. *"Fight like hell."*

I *was* fighting! Couldn't they all see that? I fought even as I crawled, my fingers so raw now, they'd gone numb.

And still I crawled until I was in the center of the clearing, my eyes locked on Eta's athame. I reached for it, sobs racking my body.

"Please," I said, my gaze going to NeeCee where she was tied to the tree. NeeCee shook her head, her eyes wide as my hand closed over the athame's handle.

I sobbed.

I sobbed, and I cursed.

I cursed Eta. I cursed myself. I cursed Lilith, and I cursed everyone in the clearing for not saving me. Once more, my eyes went to Luther. He said he'd fight his mother, so why didn't he?

A million thoughts bombarded me, like a broken image from a damaged reel of old film. Even as I stood, even as I began to open the brown bags at my feet, I wanted to laugh. Even my thoughts were like old black and white movies. Lucas' voice was in my head. *"Your family sold a soul to Lilith by summoning her. Whatever soul she pleases. It means that by helping you, all of us are breaking the rules. It means that right now, as much as we all hate to admit it, Luther is your best chance."*

I stood. There was no need to cleanse the circle. Nothing positive was going to happen here, so I marched instead, drawing a circle in the soil with the tip of Eta's athame.

Bernice whimpered against her gag, and my vision blurred once more with tears.

To the middle of the Circle, I moved, plunging the athame into the ground as I lifted the four pouches.

Out of one brown bag, I lifted two bound feathers.

Again, my body moved, lowering the feathers into one quarter of the Circle. Air. The feathers represented air.

"Oh, Monroe," Dayton breathed.

I barely heard her over Lilith's whispered demands.

"Please," I begged.

Lilith laughed.

Lucas' words echoed. *"It means that right now, as much as we all hate to admit it, Luther is your best chance."*

Luther.

I looked up again, my eyes finding his as my body moved once more to the Circle's center. Another bag. In this one, rock salt. Earth. The salt represented Earth.

Another quarter of the Circle, the salt sprinkled, my body once more in the center. And all Luther did was stare, his face still unreadable. The heat of tears against my cheeks was getting old.

I closed my eyes. What was the point in looking when my body wasn't even my own any more. Another bag. A bowl.

I kept my eyes shut. I knew this bowl. It was the same one Eta has used to represent water. And as I lowered this into yet another of the Circle's quarters, I felt my heart grow cold.

"No!"

This time when I felt my body start to return to the center of the Circle, I threw myself on the ground, my fingers once more in the soil.

"Oh no, Monroe! You can't stop now," Lilith's gleeful voice said in my head. My arms and legs shook, and I screamed again. I screamed until my throat was raw and my voice was hoarse.

Lilith laughed.

"Please!" I heard Dayton beg.

No one else said anything.

And as my body was dragged by Lilith's power once more to the center of the Circle, more thoughts plagued me. *"It means that right now, as much as we all hate to admit it, Luther is your best chance,"* Lucas had said.

My hands closed over the final brown bag.

"Tell my son this is a war even he can't win. Thorns are only good if they come attached to a rose," Lilith's voice echoed.

In my palm, there fell a fire opal. It wasn't a flame, but the jewel represented the element of fire all the same. Fire. Luther. *"Tell my son this is a war even he can't win. Thorns are only good if they come attached to a rose."* The fire opal fell to the final quarter of the Circle.

For the last time, I returned to the center, my hand going to the athame's black handle. My fingers wrapped around it, and I pulled it from the soil.

There was screaming and when I looked up, I saw that Bernice had come untied, her body dragged by some invisible force toward the Circle, lifting so it would leave the Circle's boundary untouched before she landed at my feet.

A tear caught on the edge of my chin before dripping onto NeeCee's upturned head. The athame lifted.

"No, Monroe!" NeeCee begged. "Please."

Lilith's commands ran furiously through my head. And with them, other words. *Luther is your best chance. Thorns are only good if they come attached to a rose. Luther. Thorne.*

My eyes widened, and my head lifted, my gaze going one final time to the Demon at the edge of the forest. Luther. Thorne.

My mouth began to move, repeating the same chant Eta had once said long ago. I held the athame steady, the blade gleaming in the moonlight. Eta. My heart broke all over again, and I looked down at NeeCee.

Bernice's eyes were swollen, her nose red as I chanted, and I kept my gaze on hers as the athame lowered. I lifted my hand, running the blade across my palm. Blood fell to the ground.

And in that final moment, I made a choice. I made a choice that would change my life forever.

I looked up, and with every bit of strength I had left in me, I fought Lilith's commands, a cold sweat breaking out along my skin as I summoned the only other Demon I knew.

"Thorne!"

Chapter 25

I often day dream in black and white. Everything just looks prettier with no color. Cleaner, more glamorous. I used to think this made me an optimist, envisioning life as I wanted it be rather than what it is. Now, I wonder if it just makes me afraid to face reality. I need to quit running away from my life and face it.

~Monroe's Totally Wicked Book of Shadows~

I collapsed, my body falling on top of NeeCee's even as Lilith roared.

The energy in the Circle changed, and the pain in my head vanished. I tried lifting my head, and failed.

"Monroe," a voice said.

NeeCee sat up beneath me, her hand going to my chin, and she lifted my face. Across from us in the Circle was Luther, his eyes blood red, a soft smile on his face. It was the kindest expression I'd ever seen on him, and I sagged again.

"What have you done?" NeeCee whispered.

Lilith screamed.

Luther laughed. "Seems the Ayers have a new Demon consort," he said. "Get out of my Circle, Mother."

There were other voices then. Dayton's and Marcas. And images.

Blurred images.

"Monroe," NeeCee whispered.

A cool hand touched my forehead. Someone shook me. Blackness.

And then ... air. I was being lifted, one strong arm under my head and another under my legs. My eyes opened, and Luther filled my vision.

His head lowered. "You did good, Monroe."

He pulled me into him, and I didn't fight him, my head going to his chest, my fist gripping his t-shirt.

"Why didn't you help me?" I asked weakly.

Luther's grip on me tightened. "Because this time, Monroe, you had to help yourself."

My throat constricted, and I pulled away just long enough to look up at him one final time.

"You knew all of this would happen? You knew I would summon you?" I asked.

One corner of Luther's lip lifted. "I know my mother well, Witch. I'm often accused of thinking like her. I didn't know if you would summon me, but it was the only chance we had." His head lowered, and he winked at me. "I had total confidence in you."

I fought the smile and lost, my cracked lips lifting. "And Marcas and Dayton?"

Again Luther winked. "To witness it all. So that Lilith couldn't claim your family still belonged to her. She wouldn't have had much of a claim considering your aura is probably eat up with me now. But she has considerable power in Hell. It never hurts to play it safe."

My head went back to his chest. "Luther Craig playing it safe?" I mumbled into his shirt.

I felt the rumble when he laughed all the way to the tips of my toes. Luther's body heated, and my eyelids grew heavy. I yawned.

A hand touched my hair. I tried looking up and couldn't.

"It's okay, Roe," Dayton's voice said suddenly. "Just know I came, okay? Just know I came, and that I will always come."

I tried to answer her, but my lips wouldn't move. My eyes felt glued shut.

"Is she going to be okay?" another voice asked. It was NeeCee's. She sounded scared.

"She's going to be fine," Luther answered her.

Now that it was all over, my body hurt. There was pain, *lots* of pain. Burning pain. Raw pain. And then ... sweet blackness.

Chapter 26

When I went to the river this morning, the water was churning angrily. There were no clouds in the sky, nothing to suggest a storm was coming, but there it was, an angry whirlpool. It looked like an evil eye staring up at me. It can only mean one thing. Something is coming.

~Monroe's Totally Wicked Book of Shadows~

When I woke next, I wasn't in the Salem Woods any more, I wasn't in Henry's house. I wasn't even in Salem. I was in the small bedroom in New Orleans, Louisiana I had shared with NeeCee before she'd done the power swap spell and before Luther had shown up. Before everything had gone to hell.

The room was a mess. There were clothes everywhere. The white, restored armoire that sat in the corner was hanging open with mardi gras beads dangling off of it, and the sun from a nearby window shone onto a side table holding a bowl of what I hoped was chicken broth. There was the sound of traffic below along with clomping horses and shouting pedestrians.

I tried sitting up and almost screamed.

"I wouldn't do that if I were you," my aunt's voice said, and I looked up to find Clara leaning against the open door, NeeCee peering under her arm. Belle stood over Clara's shoulder.

"You have a cracked rib, a concussion, and a million other little wounds that are going take quite a bit of time to heal," Clara added.

She moved into the room and Belle and NeeCee followed.

I looked down at the bed. "How did I get here?" I asked.

NeeCee moved the chicken broth to the floor and used the side table as a seat, scooting in close, her eyes bright.

"You've been out for two days, Monroe. Luther flew you here. The rest of us followed."

I tried sitting up again. My side protested, and I grit my teeth as I pressed my hand against the bed. Belle rushed over, propping an extra pillow behind my back.

I glanced at the door. "And where are they now? Luther and Lucas? Dayton and Marcas?"

NeeCee patted my hand on the bed. "Dayton and Marcas went back to the Outer Levels of Hell. Dayton told me to tell you to remember Tahiti and Bahama Mama drinks? And she gave me this." NeeCee handed me a pineapple flavored dumdum lollipop, and I grinned. Only Dayton. "I hope you don't mind me saying this," NeeCee added. "But you two are weird."

I laughed, and then regretted it, my hand going to my side.

Belle looked down at me, her eyes serious. "Lucas and Luther left. They didn't say where."

I looked past Bernice to the open window. A soft breeze was moving through it, lifting the corner of a purple scarf NeeCee thought looked cute hanging along the window's frame.

"And the grimoire?" I asked.

It was Aunt Clara who answered me. "It's safe. Back downstairs in the store."

My eyes moved to hers. "So you got the shop fixed then?"

Clara laughed. "Mostly. It's a work in progress."

"And she's scaring every construction worker working on the project with possible curses if they don't finish within two weeks," another voice said.

I nearly jumped out of the bed.

"Mom!"

Marissa Jacobs smiled as she stepped into the room, her usual loose, bright purple dress swinging around her legs as she moved to my bed.

She kneeled. "You think I'd let you heal alone? When you said you wanted to work with Clara's Coven on your Demonic connection, I certainly wasn't expecting this, Ellie." She fingered the edge of my shirt covering a bandage around my ribs. "NeeCee and Belle filled us in on everything that happened."

My eyes met hers. "Then you know about the Ayers?"

Mom nodded. Her gaze went to Clara's. "Looks like there's a lot about our family we need to learn, a lot about our family we should have already known. So many lives could have been saved."

I pushed myself up a little higher, wincing as I did. "But, Mom, it's going to be fine. The Ayers aren't being controlled by Lilith anymore."

Everyone looked at each other, their gazes grave.

"What?" I asked.

It was NeeCee who looked me in the eye. "But, Monroe, you still summoned a Demon. It wasn't Lilith, but ..." She let her words trail off before looking away.

I felt the muscles in my jaw tighten. Anger filled me.

"You're free now NeeCee. You're *free*. The Hunter curse was all Lilith. Now that we're not under her control. You're free."

NeeCee leaned over, her eyes filling with tears. "But you?" she said.

I shook my head, a small smile on my face. "It's okay. It's just a different kind of free."

Clara swiped at her cheeks before stomping a foot. "Okay, enough of all of that. We have work to do, and Monroe needs to rest."

NeeCee leaned over and hugged me lightly, and Belle squeezed my shoulder before they moved to the door.

"Go," Clara ordered, and she ushered them through before throwing me a smile, her gaze going to my mom's before she finally left.

Mom leaned over me, her hand finding mine on the blanket. "You did the right thing. It was the only thing you could have done in the moment. We'll find a way to get you free."

I turned my hand over, my fingers entwining with hers, and squeezed.

"Mom, really, it's going to be fine. I'm glad it happened."

Mom's eyes widened.

I smiled. "I've learned a lot about myself this past week, and surprisingly, I don't hate it."

Mom looked away, taking a deep breath before her gaze returned to mine. "You need to rest," she said. "Clara has a friend who's a doctor. He came to see you here, and we gave you something for pain before taking you for an x-ray. He left a prescription for you."

She held up a bottle, and I waved it away. "I really don't want it, Mom."

Mom gave me a look and opened the bottle before tapping a pill into her hand.

"Take it," she said. "For me, okay?"

I searched her eyes before taking the pill and placing it on my tongue. She handed me a glass of water, and I swallowed it.

"I'll be downstairs if you need me," Mom said.

She stood and patted my hand one more time before moving to the door.

"I'll be fine, Mom," I assured her.

She smiled, a troubled look behind her eyes, and disappeared down the stairs.

I stared back at the window, my eyes on the flying scarf, the traffic below making me drowsy.

Honk, honk.
Clomp, Clomp.
And then nothing.

♦ ♦ ♦

Something woke me, and when I opened my eyes, it was dark, the window still open, the sounds below quieter, less busy. I let my head roll to the side, my eyes moving to a round Mickey Mouse clock hanging on the wall that NeeCee claimed her mother had put in when she was a baby. I knew for a fact Bernice had bought it two years ago in a Disney store. The clock read 6 p.m.

My body tingled, and I grinned.

"Of course. Only you'd time your entrance on the sixth hour."

My head rolled back to the window. Just inside the room, his hand braced on the window's frame stood Luther Craig, his gleaming eyes bright in the darkness, a leather trench coat brushing the floor, the moon behind his head.

"I do like an entrance," he said.

He moved toward me, his gait confident, strong. My heart sped up.

"Can you see inside my head again?" I asked.

Luther kneeled, one of his knees going to the floor next to the bed.

"Do you want me to?" I shook my head, and he grinned. "Then no. I think you've earned your right for me to remain outside of it. For now."

He leaned over the bed, and I held my breath.

"You look like a mess," Luther said.

I laughed. "Way to make a girl feel better."

Luther chuckled. "I didn't say you looked bad. I said you looked a mess."

My eyes met his. "There's a difference?"

Luther's hand went to my cheek, his face lowering until our noses touched. "For me, there is."

His lips met mine, his hand going into my hair, and I wrapped my fingers around his bicep, my fingernails making small half-moons in his skin.

It was over too quick, and when I re-opened my eyes, he was once again by the window, his hand on the frame.

"What now?" I asked.

Luther ducked through the opening, his blood red eyes on my face.

"Remember when I said I had no interest in usurping power like my brother?" I nodded. He grinned. "I've changed my mind. Now, we go to war with Lilith."

And with that he was gone.

Epilogue

Slowly, carefully, I leaned over and pulled a ragged composition notebook out from underneath my bed. On the cover, in childish script, were the words, *Monroe's Totally ~~Rockin'~~ Wicked Book of Shadows.* It was my own personal grimoire. I didn't write in it often, and when I did, it was usually short musings, things probably only I'd understand. There was still at least ten pages in it despite the fact that I'd started this particular book of shadows when I was thirteen, but I had no plans to write anything more.

I flipped to the last words I'd written before Luther showed up in my aunt's store.

It can only mean one thing. Something is coming.

I closed it again and leaned over, pulling a clean unused leather bound journal my mother had bought for me two years back from under my bed. I kept telling myself I was going to start writing in it, but something always stopped me. It didn't feel right. The old composition book had seemed fine. Had seemed enough. Until now.

Opening the journal, I placed a fine point pen against the inside cover.

Monroe : A Book of Shadows

And then ...

This week, I discovered many of the women in my family were cursed, forced into serving the she-Demon Lilith. They became lilims, drawing their own blood generation after generation in her name.

This week, I banded together with an old ally, the Demon son of Lilith, and fought for the Ayers' freedom.

This week, I fell in love with a ghost, a man named Mac, whose courage in death will haunt me forever.

This week, I became an Ayers.

This week, I became a witch.

This week, I summoned the Demon Thorne.

This week, I became a brand new me.

About The Author

R. K. Ryals is a scatterbrained mother of three whose passion is reading whatever she can get her hands on. She makes her home in Mississippi with her husband, three daughters, a Shitzsu named Tinkerbell, and a coffeepot she *couldn't* live without. Visit her at
http://www.rkryals.com

Also Available by R.K. Ryals

<u>The Redemption Series</u>
Redemption
Ransom
Retribution

<u>The Acropolis Series</u>
The Acropolis
The Labyrinth

<u>The Scribes of Medeisia series</u>
Mark of the Mage

Printed in Poland
by Amazon Fulfillment
Poland Sp. z o.o., Wrocław